"I hope this proves something to you," Mark said seriously.

Erin stared at him blankly. "What?"

"That you need me."

"I don't suppose I should remind you that if you hadn't been here, I'd never have been locked in the bathroom in the first place?"

"You're right," he agreed. "It's beneath a princess to be cruel to a man who's just rescued her. I think you're supposed to bestow knighthood on me or something like that."

"You're lucky I don't have you locked away in the tower," Erin muttered.

"On what charge?"

"Princesses don't need formal charges," she said airily. "It's enough that you're bothering me."

Suddenly his lips curved up in a pleased smile. "That's quite an admission," he said huskily as his lips swooped down to claim hers . . .

Sherryl Woods

Sherryl Woods has been a journalist, a television critic, a travel editor, and the coordinator of an employee program at a university medical center in Miami. She's climbed endless steps in an assortment of European castles, bounced over rural Jamaican roads on a motorcycle, and negotiated a few mountainous, hairpin curves in this country, all in search of the perfect settings for romance. However, she's found that the location doesn't matter a bit if the hero by your side is intelligent, funny, sensual and, most of all, sensitive.

Dear Reader:

What could be lovelier than a day in June? The next six SECOND CHANCE AT LOVE romances, of course! Jeanne Grant sets the tone by indirectly asking: Have you ever sympathized with the "other man" in romances? The guy who's nice, but ... well, he's just not the hero. Does he ever find the woman of his dreams? In *No More Mr. Nice Guy* (#340), Jeanne Grant shouts a resounding "Yes!" You see, Alan Smith is a wonderful guy, and Carroll's deeply in love with him. But sometimes she wishes he were just a little less ... well, less predictable, cautious, and controlled! And when Alan sets out to be dashing, macho, and reckless—watch out! With humor and insight, Jeanne once again creates a hero and heroine you'll simply adore ... and a one-of-a-kind love story that you'll savor and remember...

Next, Katherine Granger shows her admirable versatility in *A Place in the Sun* (#341), in which brooding, embittered Rush Mason is hired as groundskeeper by Libby Peterson, the ladylike owner of a Cape Cod inn. As Rush's powerful presence seems to shrink the lush acreage of Libby's seaside estate, their heated glances lead to sultry, sexually charged encounters that will make your own skin prickle! Slowly the tension builds ... the mystery about Rush deepens. Here's steamy reading for a warm, melting June afternoon.

What woman hasn't dreamed of meeting a dashingly handsome, thoroughly princely man who will sweep her off her feet and take her "away from all this"? In Sherryl Woods's latest romance, *A Prince Among Men* (#342), this secret desire is fulfilled for actress-mime Erin Matthews ... and the wisdom of "Be careful what you wish for because it might come true" takes on a whole new meaning! Mysterious Mark Townsend's majestic courtship of Erin will tickle your funny bone and tug on your heartstrings.

In an inspired move, Jan Mathews unites erotic dancer Cindy Marshall from her previous romance *Slightly Scandalous* (#226) and vice-squad cop Brad Jordan from *Shady Lady* (#306) to bring you another sassy, sexy romance—*Naughty and Nice* (#343). Though Cindy's now a respectable social worker, she can't forget that she once stripped for a living—and she *won't* get involved with a man as unsuitable as Brad Jordan! Easier said than done—because Brad storms all her defenses ... and in record time! No one creates tough guys like Jan Mathews ... and no one else could have written a romance as wacky and wonderful as *Naughty and Nice*.

Next, Linda Raye returns after a long hiatus with *All the Right Moves* (#344), in which two strong-willed characters find themselves on opposite sides of an issue ... and in constant disagreement over their romantic future! Basketball coach Ryan McFadden, who simply oozes sexuality, knows at once that referee Lauren Nickels is the woman for him. But Lauren's determined to remain aloof—no matter how roguish his charm or penetrating his insight! Still, Ryan sees that beneath her tough exterior there lies a woman's secret longing. With such great ingredients for romance, it's only a matter of executing all the right moves before love triumphs.

Kelly Adams has a special talent for capturing the spirit of America's heartland—both the richness of the land and the simple honesty of the people. In *Blue Skies, Golden Dreams* (#345), city slicker Sara Scott arrives on Joe Dancy's Iowa farm intending to rescue her sister from what she considers his con-artist clutches. But with lighthearted teasing, indomitable integrity, and stubborn persistence, Joe sets Sara to baking cookies and going fishing ... turning her into a country girl and stampeding her emotions in one fell swoop! In Joe's conquest of Sara, Kelly Adams conveys a breath-catching tenderness and a reaffirmation of good living that makes your heart sing.

Have a terrific June, everyone! Warm wishes,

Ellen Edwards

Ellen Edwards, Senior Editor
SECOND CHANCE AT LOVE
The Berkley Publishing Group
200 Madison Avenue
New York, NY 10016

SHERRYL WOODS
A PRINCE AMONG MEN

A
SECOND CHANCE AT LOVE
BOOK

To Nancy and Dot
for your enthusiasm, your support,
and your love . . . this one's for you

With thanks...

To the city of New York,
for providing excitement, diversity,
and a little bit of magic.

And to Denise and Leslie
for helping me to write about it
and for so much more.

A PRINCE AMONG MEN

- *1* -

THE BRIGHT YELLOW taxi, proudly bearing the typical scrapes and dents of Manhattan's traffic wars, screeched to a halt in front of the Metropolitan Museum. Already there were scores of people scattered along the steep front steps of the impressive building, some of them students carrying on intense philosophical debates, others simply enjoying the crisp air and bright sunshine as they waited for the museum to open. Vendors lined the edge of Fifth Avenue, selling everything from roasted chestnuts and hot dogs to soft pretzels and ice cream. A juggler tossed a quartet of green and purple balls higher and higher amid the awed gasps and applause of a dozen small children and their parents.

Just up the block a group of street musicians filled the morning air with the soft strains of Bach as artists began to set up their displays of watercolors and sketches. Even Central Park contributed to the festive

1

atmosphere, its towering old trees offering up a vivid rainbow of burnt orange, red, and yellow against the clear blue of the autumn sky.

As Erin Matthews alighted from the cab, her eyes sparkled with delight at the colorful scene. As much as she hated getting out of bed at what she considered the uncivilized crack of dawn, she loved coming here on Saturday mornings, and she rarely missed a week.

"Thanks, Josh," she said, grinning as she slammed the taxi door. "You're an angel."

The burly, bearded driver, whose head nearly scraped the ceiling of the cab, scowled back at her with feigned ferocity. "A couple more of these insane races across town and we're both going to end up as angels," he grumbled. "What's the big deal about getting up fifteen minutes earlier?"

"It's the principle. No human being should have to get up before nine o'clock on a Saturday morning," she retorted brightly. "Besides, who do you think you're kidding? You love pretending you're on the Indianapolis Speedway. I'm just your excuse."

Josh's face creased with a guilty grin, and he gazed at her fondly.

"You may have a point there, kiddo," he admitted. "But if Maureen ever finds out I'm driving like some spaced-out teenager, she'll have my hide. And yours," he added pointedly.

Erin knew he was right. Her older sister had a fiery temper and a whole set of chipped "unbreakable" dishes to prove it. She was also a protective mother hen where her beloved husband and brood of kids were concerned. It had taken Josh weeks to convince her that driving a taxi in New York City was not sheer madness. He'd won his case only after broadly hinting that the alternative was speedway driving. Maureen would indeed go through the roof if she discovered that Erin was encouraging her husband to indulge his thwarted desire to be a race car driver, albeit in limited fashion.

"I won't tell if you don't," she promised solemnly, crossing her heart in a gesture of good faith.

Josh's eyes twinkled merrily. "Okay, kid. It's a deal. You need a lift home this afternoon?"

"If it's no trouble."

"You know it's not. See you around four." He gave her a cheerful thumbs-up sign as he sped off.

Erin sighed as she watched him go, wondering once more if her big sister had any idea just how lucky she was. Josh, despite his teasing remarks and grumbling complaints about his domineering wife, adored Maureen. He'd fallen in love with her when he was fifteen and she was a freckle-faced twelve-year-old with braids and braces. His loyalty and affection had never wavered, eventually embracing the entire Matthews clan as well.

To the then six-year-old Erin he had seemed a gentle giant with a heart of pure gold. Much later, when she'd wanted desperately to study acting, it had been Josh who'd scraped together the money her parents couldn't afford and sent her to college. She had vowed to repay him, and it was that determination that brought her to the museum each weekend.

Her weekday acting assignments barely covered her own living expenses and acting classes. She could have used the extra money from these Saturday street performances herself, but the proceeds were strictly for Josh. She kept them in a yellow piggy bank on her kitchen countertop, and each time the change totaled one hundred dollars, she deposited it in a savings account set up in his name.

Although the income was important, she'd also realized that working as a mime was an excellent way to hone her powers of observation. In a single day she could capture dozens of different characterizations and moods without once opening her mouth. During the week she relied on the writers' dialogue to create her occasional roles in commercials and even rarer bit parts in the soaps, but out here she was on her own, with nothing more than her slim, flexible body and mobile features as tools. And she was good at it. Damn good.

Dressed from head to toe in black, her long brown hair twisted into a knot on top of her head and hidden beneath a jaunty red beret, her cheeks brightened with an exaggerated coating of rouge, and her eyes emphasized with mascara and liner, Erin wandered toward the juggler and his crowd. Winking at Ted, she proceeded to mimic his movements with an imaginary set of balls. Used to the game but seemingly oblivious to it, Ted quickly picked up the pace of his performance, tossing his balls higher and faster, as she pretended to struggle to keep up, her face, like his, a study in concentration.

Soon, to the thorough delight of the crowd, Erin appeared to miss first one ball and then the next, her expression increasingly frustrated. When Ted began to "catch" her imaginary balls and juggle them along with his real ones, the crowd howled its approval. Scowling at them, Erin removed her hat and, stepping neatly into Ted's path, scooped one colorful ball after another from the air until Ted had none left and she strolled victoriously off with all of them. Appearing desolate, he trailed after her, until finally, with the crowd urging her on, she sadly returned the entire assortment—real and imaginary—to him.

The routine never failed to please the onlookers, who demonstrated their appreciation by dropping quarters and even an occasional dollar bill into the box Ted left open on the sidewalk. Later, as always, he would share the money with Erin.

For the next few hours she continued to perform along the street, choosing those she imitated with care, never wanting to embarrass anyone who seemed too shy to enjoy her teasing. She feigned munching on hot dogs, pretended to cry when the balloon she supposedly carried burst, and seated herself in the midst of a heated discussion on the museum steps and mimicked the participants' expressions.

It was close to four o'clock, and her body was beginning to ache, when she spotted a heart-stoppingly gorgeous man strolling purposefully toward her along Fifth Avenue, his Gucci leather briefcase and Brooks Brothers suit outward testaments to his success. With his neatly trimmed, wheat-colored hair glittering gold in the rapidly fading sunlight, and with his graceful athlete's stride, he was too perfect, too polished for Erin to resist.

She watched breathlessly as he passed by; then, without a moment's hesitation, she fell quickly into character behind him. Much to the amusement of the crowd, who'd watched with interest as she approached her latest quarry, she easily matched his no-nonsense demeanor, the squaring of his broad shoulders, and his long-legged stride. Apparently hearing the titters of the onlookers, he quickly caught on that something was going on behind him and glanced over his shoulder. Erin caught a brief glimpse of dancing gray eyes before she imitated his movement and glanced over her own shoulder, expressing similar puzzlement.

Suddenly he stopped in mid-step, and she almost slammed into him before coming to an exaggerated halt herself. He scowled down at her. She scowled back. He took a step. She matched it. As he taunted her at her own game, the sound of appreciative laughter drifted after them.

Never had anyone so easily fallen in with Erin's act; that this particular man had chosen to surprised her. Based on his neat-as-a-pin business attire on a lovely Saturday afternoon that was just right for jogging suits or jeans, she had assumed he was far too serious and intense to even have a sense of humor, much less this apparent playful streak.

Glancing up through her lashes, she caught sight of the dangerous glint of mischievous laughter in his eyes just seconds before he unexpectedly scooped her off her feet and into his arms. As though she were weightless and this were an everyday occurrence, he continued briskly on his way down Fifth Avenue, the sound of applause following them.

"Put me down," she hissed in his ear.

"Why?" he inquired with mild but seemingly genuine curiosity. "After all, you're the one who started this game."

"It's not a game," she responded indignantly.

"What would you call it then?" Slate-gray eyes mere inches from her own studied her closely, and Erin felt herself flushing under their warm intensity. Somehow the man had turned the tables on her entirely, and she didn't like it one bit. She'd merely been performing her usual act, and now she'd wound up in the arms of a madman whose firm, sensual lips were twitching with barely restrained mirth.

"It's my work," she retorted.

"Odd job, if you ask me."

"Nobody asked you. Now, put me down this instant, before I scream my head off," she warned.

"And ruin the act?" he taunted. "Your public obviously respects your silence. Besides, New Yorkers are notoriously slow to come to anyone's rescue."

"Then you agree I need rescuing?"

"Not from me. I'm just an innocent bystander who fell madly in love with a beautiful brown-haired, brown-eyed witch who cast a spell over me. I'm taking her off to my kingdom," he said, sounding amazingly serious despite the utter absurdity of the remark.

"I don't want to go to your damned kingdom," Erin protested futilely, wincing as she realized she had fallen neatly into his trap. If she started talking about kingdoms and such, he'd be certain she was just as loony as he. She decided to try again, using what she hoped was a perfectly reasonable argument that would appeal to his sense of decency—assuming, of course, that he had one.

"I want to go back and get my money before someone steals it."

She realized that for several minutes now she hadn't said a word about being put down. The discovery that she was beginning to enjoy the feel of this man's strong arms and solid chest was more than a little disturbing. He apparently guessed exactly what she was thinking because he was regarding her now with a thoughtful, amused gleam in his entrancing eyes. Tension crackled in the air between them, tension born of a primitive, elemental awareness.

"I suppose you do have a point," he conceded at last. "It would be a shame to take you off to my kingdom without your dowry."

"My dowry?" she echoed weakly.

"Of course. You wouldn't expect me to marry a princess with no dowry, would you?"

"Aren't you mixing your fairy-tale characters just a bit? First I'm a witch—"

"Only an expression, I assure you."

"—and now I'm a princess?"

"A bewitching princess," he agreed softly in a smooth-as-whiskey voice that was strangely intoxicating. Erin felt her temperature soar in the most exhilarating—and confusing—way.

"You're crazy," she announced firmly, trying not to notice that he seemed hurt by her observation.

"Is that any way to talk about the man you're going to marry?"

"Probably not. But since I have absolutely no intention of marrying you, I stand by the comment. Now, would you please put me down?" she pleaded again just as she spotted Josh's cab pulling to the curb in front of the museum. "If you don't we're going to have a rather nasty little scene on our hands in a moment, and that really would spoil the act."

The man followed her gaze and saw Josh emerging from the taxi, a scowl of outrage on his face, his huge hands balled into angry fists.

"Your husband?"

"Brother-in-law," she said tersely.

He nodded, seemingly pleased by the information and not at all intimidated by the hurried approach of a six-foot four-inch, two hundred-pound ex-linebacker who looked prepared to kill.

"Hi," he said easily, his calm, friendly demeanor stopping Josh in his tracks. Suddenly uncertain, Josh blinked and looked at Erin for some hint of what behavior she expected from him in this bizarre situation. She shrugged as the man carefully lowered her to her feet and held out his hand to her brother-in-law. "Mark Townsend."

Josh stared back at him blankly for several seconds, again looked to Erin for instructions, then finally shrugged and shook hands. "Josh Lawrence." He glared down at Erin, as though he'd just realized that he'd very nearly made a fool of himself because of her. "I thought you might be in trouble," he said accusingly.

"Mr. Townsend just got caught up in my performance and decided to change the ending a bit," she explained dryly.

"I see," Josh said, though she could tell he didn't see at all. He studied Mark Townsend intently, and, Erin noticed, the man didn't flinch for a second under Josh's protective scrutiny. Instead, some instinctive flash of masculine understanding seemed to pass between them.

Feeling ignored and inexplicably irritated, she stalked off, muttering angrily under her breath. A big help Josh was! He had changed sides without batting an eye. The traitor would probably turn her over to this total stranger without a moment's hesitation, just because he'd been telling her for months it was about time she found herself a man. She walked over to Ted, collected her share of change, then went to stand by the taxi, impatiently tapping her foot. Josh and Mark Townsend continued to chat amiably. They were probably talking football, since it was one topic Josh would discuss endlessly with almost anyone who'd listen.

Giving up on trying to send a subtle message to her brother-in-law, she climbed into the back of the cab and pointedly slammed the door. They ignored her display of temper and continued talking.

By the time they finally turned and strolled toward the cab, Erin was seething. And when Mark Townsend opened the door and climbed in beside her, she glared at him ferociously.

"What the hell are you doing?"

"I should think that would be obvious," he responded calmly, giving her a dazzling smile. With disgusting predictability, her pulse rate soared. "Your brother-in-law has offered me a lift."

"You didn't have to take it."

"But why would I refuse when it gives me a chance to get to know you better?" he countered reasonably.

She regarded him skeptically. "What's the point?"

"The usual. It always helps if you understand the woman you're going to marry."

"Stop saying that!"

"What?" he asked innocently.

"You know what."

"No, I don't. Tell me."

"Stop saying you're going to marry me. That's crazy."

"Love usually is," he said quite seriously. "Wonderfully crazy."

"That sounds suspiciously like the voice of experience. You're probably the type who falls in love at least once a day," she observed. And if that's the case, he'll be out of my life and in someone else's by this time tomorrow, she decided optimistically. Then she noticed that he was shaking his head emphatically. Her spirits sank.

"I swear to you that I have never fallen in love before in my life."

Summoning up renewed optimism, she nodded wisely. "That explains it, then."

"Explains what?"

"Why you're mistaking this momentary infatuation with love. You're walking down the street, and a woman—"

"A beautiful woman," he corrected. She scowled as she heard Josh's low chuckle from the front seat.

"—pops out of nowhere, and you think you've been enchanted. It's a perfectly reasonable reaction," she assured him soothingly, adding firmly, "but it will go away."

"I don't think so. I suspect I'm down for the count."

Erin took a deep breath and searched for yet another argument that would convince this lunatic once and for all that he was suffering from a romantic delusion. She couldn't think of one, especially since a small flutter of excitement had flared to life deep inside her. Despite all her perfectly rational protests, she found that she was responding to this very attractive man with his off-the-wall approach.

Let's face it, she admitted wryly to herself, he does have incredible, soul-searching eyes, kissable lips, a body that could advertise health clubs, and a definite, if quirky, mind of his own—a very potent, very sexy combination. She'd have to be dead not to respond. That she'd gone all weak in the knees when his leg brushed against hers didn't mean a thing. That her heart had thudded against her ribs when she was in his arms certainly didn't indicate that she could ever fall in love with him. Intelligent, rational people did not fall in love with complete strangers.

Almost timidly, Erin glanced at him and found that he was lounging comfortably next to her, looking perfectly relaxed and heedless of the turmoil raging inside her. For a man who professed that he'd neatly side-stepped romantic involvements his entire life, he seemed thoroughly at ease with the fate he had decreed for the two of them. Suddenly that seemed to her the most irritating part of all: He was taking all this in stride, while she came unglued like some nervous adolescent.

All what? her mind taunted. Was she beginning to accept the crazy notion that he had actually fallen in love with her in a split second, that destiny had thrown them together to live happily ever after? Of course not!

She shook her head and gazed pointedly out the window. Outside was reality: cars lined up bumper to bumper, horns blaring, drivers shouting; dusk descending, shrouding the city in a cloak of pale, filtered sunlight; shoppers crowded together at bus stops; store windows plastered with sale signs and displays of neon-bright clothes only teenagers would dare to wear; the pungent smells of garlic, ginger, and grease from a succession of ethnic restaurants.

Inside the cab she was caught in a dreamworld. As an actress she spent much of her time steeped in fantasy, but offstage she prided herself on being firmly rooted in reality. The balance was essential, and Mark Townsend was tipping it all out of kilter. At any moment she expected him to decree that this was a magical chariot that could whisk them away to the perfect, romantic kingdom of his imagining. Worse, she was beginning to suspect she would agree to go. One of them had to get out of this chariot—*cab!*—before things got entirely out of control.

"Josh," she began just as he pulled to a stop in front of a midtown skyscraper. Good grief, she thought, even Josh was granting wishes before she spoke them.

"Here you go, Mark," her brother-in-law said cheerfully.

"Thanks." He took one of Erin's trembling hands in his and lifted it gallantly. The fleeting brush of his warm lips against her cool skin created a feverish sensation that quickly spread.

"Bye, princess," he said, his voice husky with promise. "I'll see you soon. We have plans to make."

"Plans?"

"Sure," he said cheerfully as he got out of the taxi. "Wedding plans."

"There isn't going to be a wedding," she said, unable to keep the hint of desperation from her voice.

"Of course there is," he countered firmly. "Talk to her, Josh."

Josh shook his head. "Hey, pal, you're on your own. It took me nearly ten years to convince her sister to marry me, and Erin's even more stubborn than Maureen."

Mark gazed at Erin with feigned severity. "If you think I'm waiting ten years for you, princess, you're the one who's crazy. I might be willing to hold out for ten days, maybe two weeks, but that's my limit."

"Ten days?" Erin was getting irritated with her inability to do anything more than echo Mark's words. "I am not going to marry you! Not ten days from now, not ten months from now, not even ten years from now! I don't even know you!"

"We'll fix that," he promised soothingly. "I'll pick you up for brunch tomorrow at eleven."

"Forget it." She glared at him, stubbornly ignoring the fact that one tiny part of her—obviously an overactive gland—did want to see the wacky, silly, immensely charming Mark Townsend again. It didn't make sense, and she did not do things that didn't make sense.

Mark's lips, however, had set in an equally stubborn line. "Eleven o'clock," he repeated. Then, with a jaunty wave, he strolled off.

Erin heard Josh chuckle. "Don't you say a word, Josh Lawrence," she ordered heatedly. "Not one word."

He turned and shot her a smug grin instead.

- 2 -

WHEN THE DOORBELL rang at her studio apartment Sunday morning, Erin almost spilled a glass of tomato juice down the front of the new, outrageously expensive, pale pink Christian Dior robe she'd bought in a momentary lapse from her usual rigid frugality.

"Damn," she muttered as she hastily daubed at the red specks threatening the pastel silk. With her heart thudding against her ribs, she glanced nervously at the clock, confirming her worst fear. It was 11 A.M. On the dot.

During the night she had actually managed to convince herself that Mark Townsend would not show up. For one thing, she'd never told him her address. For another, her phone number was unlisted. She should have known the man would be resourceful. Men with Gucci briefcases usually were. And Josh had probably been disgustingly cooperative. He'd paint her phone number across a Times Square billboard if he thought it would bring the perfect man into her life.

As the doorbell chimed again, she sighed and went to answer it. Peering cautiously through the peephole, she noted that Mark's cheerful expression was rapidly giving way to an aggrieved scowl. He poked impatiently at the doorbell again.

"Okay, okay," she called out as she turned the various locks.

By the time she had the door open at last, a crooked grin was tilting Mark's lips once more. "Are you by any chance storing the overflow from Fort Knox in here?"

"No. Something even more valuable," she tossed back airily.

"Diamonds and rubies?"

"Nope. Better than that."

"Modest, aren't you?" he teased.

"Why should I be modest? I'm well aware of my own worth, preferably alive."

His expression changed with lightning swiftness from amusement to something else, something warm and caring. The intense, totally unexpected look took her breath away. She felt . . . cherished, and no one had ever made her feel that way before. It was a wonderful yet scary feeling.

"I'm glad you take care of yourself," he said softly. "It'll make my job easier."

"Your job?" she echoed, wondering if she'd lost complete control of her vocabulary along with her sanity. She'd never thought of herself as a mindless actress who couldn't string two words together without a script, but the last two days had made her begin to wonder.

"As your protector."

"Are you in the security business?" she asked, the

incredibly warm feeling of a moment ago giving way to suspicion. "Is that what this is all about? You want to sell me an alarm system? A bodyguard, maybe?"

"Of course not," he responded indignantly. "I'm going to marry you. Remember?"

How could she forget? It was not every day that a total stranger announced his intentions in such a clear, uncompromising manner.

"Look, Mark," she said softly, gazing up and meeting his intense gray eyes. That odd feeling was back again. "Um, look, I think we need to talk."

"Of course we do," he said agreeably. "That's what brunch is all about." His glance skimmed over her. "Why aren't you ready?"

Erin looked away nervously. "I didn't think you were serious," she admitted finally.

"Love, I am most definitely serious where you are concerned."

His words sounded distressingly like a solemn oath, which scared the daylights out of her. She had been pursued by any number of ardent suitors in her twenty-six years. Only one of them had caught her, and he had been a mistake, a dreadful mistake. She had thought that Terry was dependable, reliable. He had had a nine-to-five job and a steady income—things she'd thought would be the perfect balance to the unpredictability of her own life, things she'd yearned for while growing up in a household that never knew from one week to the next if there would be rent money.

They'd dated for two years, and she'd thought she knew everything there was to know about him, but Terry hadn't been at all what he seemed. He'd left work at five but disappeared for hours on end. He'd collected a weekly paycheck, then gambled it all away.

In retrospect she'd realized all the signs had been there from the first. There had been nights during their courtship when he'd been too busy to see her, though he'd offered no real explanation. There had been evenings when he was embarrassed about being short of cash and had reluctantly let her pay for dinner or a movie. She'd rationalized it all away at the time, overlooked the uncomfortable feeling she'd had when she'd picked up the check. She'd even told herself it was good that he had other interests that kept him occupied. It was only after the wedding that she'd realized what those other interests were.

They had stayed together for six months, as she tried desperately to reconcile his irresponsibility with her dream of stability. Finally she'd realized that even a love much deeper than hers could not overcome such basic differences in values, and she'd sadly said goodbye and walked out. Terry hadn't tried to stop her.

Since then she had kept men at a safe, friendly distance. With renewed determination and energy she had focused on her own career, a career that was demanding enough to fill her days, if not her nights. Despite their own ambitions, most men failed to understand her drive to succeed. To her relief, they'd been easily put off by it, leaving her life romantically uncomplicated.

However, she was forced to admit, not one of those men had displayed Mark Townsend's unyielding, if bizarre, resolve, his unwavering sense of humor, or his undeniable sex appeal. If she didn't wriggle out of this absurd situation very soon, she was going to be in so much trouble it would take the entire protective Matthews clan to extricate her—assuming, of course, that they hadn't already joined forces with Josh and decided to abandon her to the whims of this charming rogue.

Suddenly, with distressing clarity, she envisioned them all gathered around Maureen's kitchen table for Sunday brunch, clucking delightedly at Josh's news that dear little Erin had finally met her match, that at last she was putting that tragic business with Terry behind her. She had the urge to pick up the phone and call to tell them to forget it. Look what had happened with Terry, and he'd at least seemed sane. If she had to take a poll based on what she'd seen in the last twenty-four hours, nine out of ten people would agree that Mark Townsend was certifiably wacko.

"Are you okay?" Mark's voice was soft and filled with concern. "You looked funny there for a minute."

"I always look funny when I'm considering murder," she retorted.

"Murder?" For the first time, she noted with a modest amount of pleasure, he looked uncertain.

"Josh. My sister. My whole bloody family," she said wearily. "I'm thinking of killing them all."

"You think Josh told me where to find you," he said with sudden insight. "And you're upset about it."

"Now, why would that upset me?" she asked sarcastically. "My dear brother-in-law tells some total stranger—who might be a mass murderer for all he knows—where I live and then sits back and waits for a wedding announcement."

"Josh didn't tell me."

Erin blinked in confusion. "He didn't? Then how...?"

"It's not important," he said smoothly, dismissing the whole issue. "Now, how does the rest of your family fit in?"

"Wait a minute! It is important."

"I just did a little research. No big deal. Now, why

are you angry with your family?"

"What kind of research?"

"To get your address," he said, leading her right back to the beginning of the discussion. Erin wavered, then reluctantly decided to drop the subject. It was clear from the stubborn set of his lips that she wasn't going to get anywhere. Besides, what did it matter really? The point was that he was here.

"What about your family?" he prodded.

"They're probably all at Josh's house right this minute, gloating."

"About us?"

She nodded. "You're beginning to catch on."

"So, why don't we go over there and you can introduce me?"

Erin buried her face in her hands. "I should have known. I give you a scenario of my traitorous family rushing to marry us off, and you want to go join ranks with them."

He grinned at her, and her damnable heart thudded eagerly. "Of course. From what you say, they're displaying very good judgment."

"Oh?"

"Sure. They're on my side."

"Which means," she informed him tartly, "that they're not on mine."

"No, love. That's not what it means at all. They just want you to be happy."

"That's quite a jump in logic."

He shook his head emphatically. "You do admit that I want to make you happy?"

"So you say."

"And you think they're on my side?"

Erin could see exactly where he was heading. She nodded weakly.

"Ergo, they want you to be happy."

"Oh, my God," she murmured, covering her face with her hands.

"What's wrong now?"

"The way you said it, it actually sounds reasonable," she said with a note of desperation in her voice. "I must be losing my mind."

"No. You're just coming to your senses. Now, why don't you quit worrying and get dressed. I know a great place for brunch. As soon as you've had a glass of champagne and some eggs Benedict, you'll feel better."

Erin sincerely doubted it. She had a feeling it was going to take more than champagne and some poached eggs topped with hollandaise sauce to make her feel better. A few weeks of analysis or a very long vacation in the Caribbean might do it, but a mere brunch definitely would not.

Still, she decided, glancing at him cautiously, she might as well try to cope with Mark Townsend on a full stomach. Perhaps then she'd have the strength to talk him out of this insane idea of his, instead of getting weak-kneed every time he looked at her. Like now. She gulped and looked away. She had the strongest urge to hide in her bedroom until he disappeared, but he was standing in the middle of her bedroom. In her tiny studio apartment, she had absolutely no place to run except the bathroom. Taking a deep breath, she opted for that, shutting the door securely behind her.

She flipped the lock and sagged against the door. Surely she would wake up from this crazy dream soon and she would be safe and secure in her fold-out bed with the image of Mark Townsend only a dim memory. She closed her eyes. The image stayed with her in vivid Technicolor. Pale-gold hair. Gray, almost blue, eyes, fringed by thick blond lashes. Blue oxford-cloth shirt, open at the neck to reveal a hint of tan flesh. Faded, well-worn, snug jeans with a designer tag on the hip pocket. Gucci loafers in rich brown leather. Socks? Her mind drew a blank.

She drew a shaky breath. She knew exactly why she couldn't remember his socks: Her eyes had focused almost entirely on the provocative fit of those damn jeans on his flat stomach, narrow hips, and muscular legs. A liquid warmth spread through her, and, glancing in the mirror, she noticed that her cheeks were flushed, her eyes extraordinarily wide and bright. She was either coming down with a tropical disease or she was entirely too responsive to Mark Townsend. She had a feeling the disease would be easier to cure.

Turning the shower full blast, she slipped out of her robe, noticing in dismay that the dusky rose tips of her breasts had tightened into hard, sensitive buds. Her breasts ached with a desire to be touched. By Mark Townsend, no doubt. Even her body was betraying her.

"Oh, dear Lord," she moaned plaintively as she stepped beneath the sharp spray of the warm shower. "Get me out of this. I do not have time to play games with this lunatic. I certainly do not have time to fall in love."

She let the stinging water wash over her, praying it would somehow cleanse her mind of unwanted thoughts. Eventually, though, she knew it wouldn't work. There was nothing to be done about the wayward turn her emotions and body had taken. She might as well get dressed and get on with the day. Perhaps by nightfall normalcy would return. No doubt anyone as pleasantly daft as Mark appeared to be would soon grow bored by her more rational approach to life. He'd wander off and turn someone else's life upside down. A sharp tug in her chest suggested that deep inside she was not nearly as wild about that alternative as she should be.

She stepped out of the tub into the warm, steamy room. Briskly toweling herself dry, she realized that in her hurried escape from Mark's seductive presence, she'd neglected to bring along her clothes. She shrugged and piled her long brown hair loosely on top of her head. Pulling her robe tightly around her, she turned the lock on the bathroom door and tried to open it. It wouldn't budge. She tugged harder. It remained determinedly in place.

"Blast it all," she muttered. Why hadn't she remembered the damn door tended to stick the minute the bathroom steamed up? Because she'd been in no condition to think about anything except the attractive man in her living room and the effect he had on her without even trying.

She sat down on the edge of the tub and tried to think calmly. What had she done the last time the door stuck? Hell, she could barely remember the last time the door had been stuck. She'd had sense enough never to close it tightly after that one disastrous experience when she'd first moved in. Then Josh and Maureen had been in the living room, and they'd freed her.

She sighed heavily. There were two alternatives. She could stay in here until the dampness evaporated and the door was no longer swollen shut or she could swallow her pride and ask Mark for help. She might as well get it over with.

"Mark?"

"Yes?"

"Could you give me a hand?"

"Well, well," he murmured with a delighted chuckle. "You need some help drying your back?"

Suddenly the idea of staying right where she was seemed infinitely safer.

"No, you creep. I'm stuck in here. The door's jammed."

"You're kidding!"

"Mark," she said, her voice sardonic, "would I still be in here if I were kidding?"

"I'm not so sure. You seemed pretty eager to race in there a little while ago," he observed.

Erin could just imagine the amused quirk of his lips, the twinkle in his eyes. When she got out of here, she was going to get even with him for this!

"Mark!" she shouted.

"Okay. Okay," he soothed. "Just stay away from the door."

Erin sat where she was and waited. And waited. Finally, she saw the knob turn ever so slightly. The door, however, remained securely in place.

"Um, Mark," she began softly, trying to stifle a giggle. "It's stuck, remember? If merely turning the knob would do it, I'd be out of here."

"Don't rush me," he muttered darkly. "I could leave you in there."

For several long minutes there was absolute silence.

"Mark, what are you doing?" she called out just as the door trembled and shook and one Gucci loafer came crashing through, leaving splinters of wood all over the floor. A loud yelp of pain, followed by a colorful stream of obscenities, echoed through the tiny apartment. In spite of herself, Erin laughed as the foot slowly receded through the gaping hole in the lower half of the door. Glinting gray eyes, an aristocratic nose, and a stubborn mouth replaced the foot, peering in at her sheepishly.

"Nice try, hero," she murmured between giggles.

"Dry rot," he muttered.

"Should I resign myself to staying in here, or do you have another plan?"

"Don't get sassy, princess, or I'll lock you away for good."

"Sorry."

"Do you have a screwdriver?"

"What for?"

"What do you think?"

"Whoops," she said, unable to restrain her laughter. "I see the prince has a temper."

"The prince wants a screwdriver," he grumbled.

"In the kitchen. Top drawer on the right, by the stove."

She peeked through the hole in the door and saw him stalk into the kitchenette, yank open the drawer, and reach in.

"Damn! What the devil was that?" His startled shout resounded through the apartment. "Erin!"

"I guess I forgot to mention the mousetrap," she responded weakly.

"Mousetrap?" he thundered.

"A primitive form of extermination," she offered helpfully.

"I know what a mousetrap is. Why was it in the drawer set to go off?"

"Actually, it was in the kitchen closet set to go off,

but then I saw the cute little mouse one day and I couldn't bear the thought of hurting it, so I put the trap away."

"Still set," he muttered, shaking his head.

"I didn't really think about that," she responded meekly, adding brightly, "I did take the cheese out, though. I gave it to the mouse."

"You're quite a humanitarian." The way he said it didn't seem exactly complimentary, and, judging from his grim expression as he returned with the screwdriver, he was not exactly thrilled with her at the moment. She retreated to her seat on the tub to wait.

Moments later, its hinges removed, the door went tumbling down. Erin rose with as much dignity as she could manage and stepped carefully over it into the living room. Mark was regarding her expectantly.

"Thank you," she said solemnly.

"You're welcome. I hope this proves something to you."

She stared at him blankly. "What?"

"That you need me."

"I don't suppose I should remind you that if you hadn't been here, I'd never have been locked in the bathroom in the first place?"

"You're right," he agreed as she disappeared into her clothes closet. "It's beneath a princess to be cruel to a man who's just rescued her. I think you're supposed to bestow knighthood on me or something like that."

Erin muttered a retort.

"What?"

She stepped out of the closet and glared at him. "I said you're lucky I don't have you locked away in the tower."

"On what charge?"

"Princesses don't need formal charges," she said airily. "It's enough that you're bothering me."

Suddenly his expression softened, and his lips curved upward in a pleased smile. As he slowly approached her, Erin held her breath. Her brain shouted at her to run, but her feet seemed rooted to the floor. Cupping her chin in his hand, he gently tilted her face up until she was staring directly into mesmerizing gray eyes as soft and alluring as rabbit's fur.

"That's quite an admission," he said huskily as his lips swooped down to claim hers in a fleeting, tantalizing kiss.

The silky warmth was there and gone so quickly that Erin thought for a moment she'd only imagined it. But the blazing wildfire it had left inside her was real enough. Her lips parted in surprise, and she gazed quizzically up at Mark. He chuckled at her obvious astonishment.

"You're beginning to believe me, aren't you?" he teased gently, his hands resting lightly on her shoulders, burning her skin through the silk of her robe.

Erin wasn't about to pretend she didn't understand. She was also not about to admit the truth. "No," she said adamantly.

"Liar." The taunt was quiet and amused.

She blinked and broke free, gathering up her clothes and stalking off to the bathroom. Mark's deep chuckle followed her. Only after she'd stepped back across the fallen door did she realize the bathroom would offer her no privacy, no escape this time. She clutched the cool porcelain edge of the sink.

What on earth was she supposed to do now? Deep down, she knew Mark was right. He had gotten to her, and all the doors in the world wouldn't keep her out of his arms for long if that's where he wanted her to be.

That, of course, had absolutely nothing to do with her current dilemma of how to get dressed without his penetrating gaze observing every move. She glanced around, stepped decisively into the tub, yanked the still-damp curtain closed, and promptly splattered water on her clothes. She groaned as she shook them out and put them on.

- 3 -

AN HOUR LATER Erin found herself seated across from Mark in a cozy restaurant with a spectacular view of Central Park. Although the place was jammed when they arrived, within minutes they had been shown to a prime table by a window overlooking the park. The cork had been popped on a bottle of champagne and their glasses filled before she could even open her leather-bound menu.

When the waiter left, she regarded Mark closely. "Do you own stock in this place?"

"Nope."

"Come here often?"

He nodded, and a vision of other Sundays and other women flashed through Erin's mind. She wasn't wild about the accompanying reaction of pure jealousy that knotted her stomach. She should have been feeling relief. In fact, she should have been thrilled to discover that she wasn't the first and probably wouldn't be the last in a whole string of these crazy weekend adventures of Mark Townsend. Instead, she felt . . . miserable.

"Does that bother you?"

"Of course not," she denied firmly.

Mark grinned. "Does, too. You're a lousy liar. Don't ever get in trouble with the police."

"I'm a very law-abiding citizen."

"Most law-abiding citizens do not want to murder their entire families," he reminded her.

"It was an expression," she retorted. "Actually, I love my family. They're all pretty terrific people."

Mark settled back in his chair and regarded her with interest. "You obviously have at least one sister, since Josh is your brother-in-law. What about the rest?"

"Dad's a retired baker in Brooklyn. Mom has always been a housewife, though for a while she took in sewing to help make ends meet," she said matter-of-factly. Then she was surprised to find herself adding, "They were always struggling, though they tried very hard to keep it from my sister, Maureen, and me. Maureen seemed to take it in stride, but somehow I always sensed the tension around the first of the month when the rent was due and the bills came in.

"Once right in the middle of winter, they cut off our electricity. It took forty-eight hours to get it turned back on. Mom and Dad tried to make a game of it. They got out candles, and we bundled up in the living room and pretended we were camping," she recalled, shivering at the memory. Her eyes clouded over, and she added softly, "But it was awful."

Suddenly Erin was aware of exactly how much she had revealed. It was as though a dam had been opened and the words had come pouring out. This was something she never talked about. It was just the way her life had been. Perhaps her openness now had something to do with Mark's gaze. It was filled with so much compassion and understanding, such tenderness.

"That must have been pretty rough," he said gently, and suddenly all those old feelings were back, tormenting her. She had never really tried to block out the memories of those times. In fact, she had used them to fuel her determination to succeed. It had been a long time, though, since she had allowed them to make her feel quite so sad, quite so vulnerable. Embarrassed, she tried to blink away the tears that shimmered in her eyes.

"The worst part was the sadness in Dad's eyes when he looked at Mom. You could tell he thought he'd failed her. It's given me an obsession about money. I don't need a lot of it, but I'm almost fanatical about not living beyond my means and about paying my bills on the same day I get them. It ruined my marriage."

There was a flicker of surprise in Mark's eyes. "You were married?"

"Very briefly."

"But your name . . . ?"

"I changed it back to Matthews."

"So there would be nothing left to remind you," he said astutely. "You must have been pretty bitter."

"I was," she admitted, "but I got over it. I finally realized I was just as much at fault as Terry was. I thought I knew him, but it turned out I only knew the man I wanted him to be. Then I blamed him when he didn't live up to my expectations. Marriage ruined a terrific fantasy."

"I'm sorry," Mark said, sounding as if he meant it.

"So am I."

"Tell me about Maureen."

Erin's expression brightened. "Maureen is wonderful, though she has a temper that makes mine pale by comparison. Josh, fortunately, is very easygoing, so they're perfectly balanced. They have three kids, all of them holy terrors. The army could use them for survival training for new recruits. And I have enough aunts and uncles and cousins to make any holiday a rowdy affair."

"It sounds wonderful."

Erin caught the wistful note in his voice and looked at him, curious. "What about you?"

"I'm pretty much on my own. Let's order," he added tersely.

Erin was puzzled by the abrupt change of subject and the look of sadness that shadowed his normally bright eyes. "Mark?" she said gently.

"I'll tell you about my family sometime," he promised, meeting her gaze for just a moment before looking back down at his menu. "How about Swedish waffles? Or would you rather have eggs Benedict?"

Erin was oddly hurt by his sudden reticence, but there had been no mistaking the pain that had accompanied the mention of his own family life—or lack of one—and she was reluctant to force the issue. But for some reason, the idea of having secrets between them bothered her more than she would have thought possible.

Grasping somewhat desperately for a firmer hold on the reality of their casual if unusual acquaintance, she asked, "What do you do when you're not trying to lure women off to your kingdom, Mark?"

"I'm in business," he said with apparently deliberate vagueness.

Erin was beginning to get the strangest desire to shake him until more specific information fell from his lips. She'd been spilling her innermost secrets, and he wouldn't even discuss what he did for a living. It hardly seemed fair. "What kind of business?" she urged patiently.

Mark looked distinctly uncomfortable. "Actually I work . . . sort of . . . undercover."

"You're kidding! You're a cop?" The idea was absolutely mind-boggling. Undercover cops wore blue jeans and Hawaiian-print shirts and hung out with drug dealers, didn't they? Except, maybe, on *Miami Vice*, whose wardrobe designer was into seriously expensive casual wear. None of the cops she'd ever seen, undercover or not, wore three-piece suits and carried Gucci briefcases.

Mark, however, was shaking his head. "Not exactly."

"What then?"

"I'm more or less a private investigator."

This was getting more difficult to believe by the minute. As hard as she tried, she simply could not envision Mark working in a sleazy office in some dingy fifth-floor walk-up or waiting in the hallway with a camera to trap some illicit lovers with the evidence for a nasty divorce case. Maybe she'd been reading too many crime novels. Perhaps he was more like Magnum. Now, that was an intriguing thought. She looked at him with renewed interest.

"Um, what exactly do you do as a private investigator?" She was envisioning a flashy sportscar racing along the Hawaiian coastline.

"White-collar crime mostly. It seemed like an interesting way to make use of my MBA," he added lightly.

Erin tried to shift her mental image of Mark in Hawaii to one of him behind a desk in a fancy corporate skyscraper. It was a much more fitting image. It also explained the three-piece suit. On the other hand, it added to the mystery of Mark Townsend's quirky personality.

"You have an MBA and you're working as a private investigator? That's not exactly your typical career path. Shouldn't you be climbing up the corporate ladder on your way to the presidency of some conglomerate?"

"Is that what you want your husband to do?" he asked, eying her sharply.

As a matter of fact, the idea did hold a certain appeal, but Erin had the distinct feeling she shouldn't admit it. Mark seemed to regard a corporate presidency with the same degree of enthusiasm she reserved for an unbalanced checkbook. "That's not what I meant," she hedged.

"What, then?"

"I just meant that what you're doing seems to be a waste of your talents. You could be in command."

"Being in command is also traditional and boring," he retorted with an odd trace of bitterness.

"Ah," she murmured as some of the pieces fell into place. Mark Townsend would never settle for traditional. Just look at the extraordinary manner in which he'd fallen in love. No carefully planned introductions from family friends. Not even a casual pick-up in a singles bar. No, indeed. He claimed to have been bewitched by a princess in the middle of a sidewalk. Suddenly Erin's thoughts were right back where they'd started, troubling and dangerous.

"What's wrong, Erin?"

"Nothing."

"You're probably just faint from hunger. As soon as you get some food into that skinny body of yours, you'll be fine."

She glared at him. "I am not skinny," she retorted.

He grinned back at her, and her heart flipped over. "Struck a nerve, did I?"

"Of course not," she denied, recalling the countless times her mother had tried to force extra helpings of vegetables, meat, or dessert on her to try to fatten her up.

As if he were a mind-reader, Mark said, "I'll bet your mother thinks you're too skinny, too."

"Well, you're both wrong," she said frostily. "I have as many curves as the next woman."

The minute the words were out of her mouth, Erin knew the comment had been the wrong one. Mark's face split with a delighted smile, and his eyes drifted slowly and appreciatively over her, leaving a warm blush in the wake of his gaze.

"Oh, you have all the right curves, Ms. Matthews," he said seductively. "There's no doubt about that."

"So what's the problem?" she demanded defensively.

"You just look as though a strong wind might blow you away, and I'd hate to lose you to the inhabitants of Oz," he said solemnly.

Erin met his twinkling gaze and giggled in spite of herself. "You're nuts."

"You've mentioned that before. I prefer to think I have a whimsical imagination."

"So," she said triumphantly, "you admit it."

He stared at her blankly. "Admit what?"

"That you have an overactive imagination."

"Did I say that?" he asked innocently.

"You know you did."

"So what?"

"Then you must realize that all this nonsense about being in love with me is just your imagination working overtime."

He was shaking his head before she finished the sentence. "Sorry, princess. That comes from my heart, not my imagination."

"But it can't," she insisted desperately.

"Why not?"

"Because . . . because it's ridiculous. It's too soon."

"By whose standards?"

"Mine," she said, glaring at him defiantly.

He smiled at her tolerantly. "Okay, then. We'll take our time. But," he added firmly, "the end result will be the same. We're getting married, princess. Soon. I've planned every day of my ten-day campaign, and we're already on day two." His eyes twinkled merrily. "Enjoy your waffle."

Erin practically choked instead. "Mark, nobody in his right mind has a ten-day campaign to get somebody to marry him."

"Why not? If you see something you want, you have to go for it."

"Haven't you ever heard of an old-fashioned courtship?"

"Sure. But we're not old-fashioned."

"Maybe *you're* not, but I have some very specific ideas about how two people are supposed to meet, get to know each other, fall in love, and *then* get married."

"That's exactly what we're doing, princess," he said enthusiastically, as if she'd just grasped some obscure point of law and he was very proud of her. "We're just doing it fast."

Erin groaned and took another gulp of champagne. She could not cope with another minute of Mark Townsend's twisted logic. She decided to concentrate on the fluffy, tender waffle in front of her with its topping of powdered sugar and fresh strawberries. This brunch was a rare treat, and she might as well make the most of it. Maybe she could even relax and enjoy Mark's quixotic company.

But, she realized, as her gaze rose cautiously to meet his interested, speculative gleam from time to time, relaxation was next to impossible. His virile presence was a reminder of his expectations. In the long run—no, in the very short run—Mark Townsend would not be satisfied with a companion for brunch. Sooner or later he'd sworn to have her in his life—which also meant in his bed—for good. But she was not about to rush headlong into another marriage. Ten days? The very idea was absurd. It practically guaranteed disaster. She'd taken her time before marrying Terry, and look what happened to that.

Yet, at the memory of Mark's casual kiss in her apartment, a floodtide of sensations washed over her, sweeping her into imaginings of the natural progression from that tender kiss to the passion of making love, her legs entwined with his, her throbbing breasts pressed to his muscled chest, his gentle hands exploring her.

Desperately, she took another gulp of cool, sparkling champagne. The image intensified. This has to stop, she told herself emphatically, muttering a hasty excuse and rushing off to the ladies' room. Inside the gilt and marble area, she looked at herself in the mirror and shook her head. How many times in one day could you run and hide in a bathroom? Was that something they put in *The Guinness Book of World Records?* If so, she probably had a pretty good chance of capturing the title.

She gazed at herself indignantly. *No more, Erin! Running away is childish. Besides, Mark is going to be right there when you get back, so what's the point*.

"The point is that I'm scared, and these escapes give

me time to get my act together," she muttered.

The only way to get your act together is to hang in there and follow your heart.

"Easy for you to say," she told her reflection. "Give me a break."

"Did you say something, miss?" the attendant asked politely.

"No. I guess I was just talking to myself."

"Don't worry about it, dear. That happens a lot in here."

Erin smiled weakly at the woman. "I'll bet it does. Tell me, does anyone ever get any answers?"

"Beg pardon?"

"Never mind," she said, dropping some change into the dish on the vanity. "I suppose I'm on my own with this one."

By the time she returned to the table, Mark had paid the bill and was clearly ready to leave.

"How about walking back?" he suggested. "The park should be lovely."

"What about muggers?" she wondered hesitantly, her mother's repeated warnings that she should stay away from Central Park etched into her brain. "I have a very healthy instinct for self-preservation."

"Don't worry, princess," he said soothingly. "I'll be there to rescue you. That's what heroes are for."

As soon as they entered the park, Erin realized her fears had been foolish. On a Sunday afternoon, the park was hardly a deserted haven for would-be thugs. The paths were crowded with joggers, nannies pushing baby carriages, and families strolling. Some people flew kites, while others played touch football.

Couples sat on blankets under the cloudless blue sky, totally engrossed in each other. Erin looked at them enviously and wondered what it would be like to be falling in love, to be starting that exciting process of discovery. It had been so long since those first idyllic days with Terry, and no one since had really entranced her.

Until Mark, she realized with a sharp tug of awareness. She glanced sideways at him and caught him studying her.

"What are you doing?" she asked shakily.

"Watching you."

"Why?"

"Because I can't believe I've found you."

"Were you looking for me?" she taunted lightly.

"My whole life," he replied solemnly.

"Mark..." she began, planning to object, but her voice trailed off as he stopped and pulled her from the path.

"Shh," he said softly, placing a finger to her lips. "Don't fight me on this. We were meant to be. I knew it the instant I saw you."

"How did you know?" Erin asked breathlessly as his fingers traced a delicate path along her neck, where she was sure he could feel her racing pulse.

"I'm not sure," he admitted slowly. "Something in your eyes, maybe. Or the way a strand of your silky brown hair had fallen loose and curled down along your cheek. Or it could have been the way you moved, so graceful, so ladylike, yet with such sensuality. Maybe it was just that you seemed like such fun, a free spirit who lives for the moment. Like me."

Erin was thunderstruck. "You saw all that in me in just a few minutes?"

"In a split second," he corrected solemnly.

Eyes wide, she gazed at him wordlessly, wondering

what on earth she was supposed to do now. A slow smile tilted the corners of his mouth, and for the first time she noticed that he had a tiny dimple that gave him an impish, endearing look. Tentatively, she reached out and touched the intriguing indentation.

Mark captured her hand and brought it to his lips, kissing each finger in turn, then the sensitive palm. His eyes never left hers, and Erin began drowning in those gray pools of desire. She was floating, drifting away on the gently spinning whirlpool of sensations created by his touch.

"I want to kiss you," he said softly.

Yes! a traitorous inner voice shouted even as Erin was shaking her head. If he kissed her, she would be lost, caught up in the fantasy. They had to have time, had to get to know each other in the real world. She needed stability, reliability. Mark was fun, crazy, absolutely nuts. Was it at all possible that underneath that wacky exterior there was the sane, rational man she needed? She had to know before she could make the kind of commitment he was demanding. Today had given her only hints, when what she needed was concrete evidence.

His eyes met hers and held her gaze; then, apparently finding what he sought, he nodded in satisfaction. "Okay," he said agreeably, taking her hand and walking on. "When you're ready." He grinned. "We have eight days left."

Erin's heart fluttered nervously. Eight days! He actually meant to overcome every one of her reservations in little more than a week. One minute the idea panicked her; the next, with a shiver of anticipation, she simply wondered how he planned to pull it off. She decided it was better not to think about it at all.

They walked the rest of the way to her apartment in silence. Erin suddenly realized that, except when he was talking about getting married, she was beginning to feel amazingly comfortable with this man who'd wandered into her life just the day before. His gently prodding had encouraged her to talk about ghosts she'd needed to exorcise long ago. His calm reaction to her past, his understanding without the slightest sign of pity, which she would have found intolerable, made her feel closer to him than she'd felt to many men she'd known much longer. In fact, the only time she'd felt any real distance between them had been when they'd been talking about his family.

"Mark," she said abruptly when they reached her doorstep, "tell me about your family."

His eyes clouded over again, just as they had earlier, and his lips settled into a stubborn line.

"I can't. Not yet," he said softly, dropping a swift kiss on her forehead. Then to her astonishment, he walked away without another word.

Erin wanted to shout after him, "Why not? Is there a wife already at home? A lover? A convicted felon lurking on some limb of the family tree? What?" But something distinctly forbidding in Mark's suddenly shuttered eyes as he had turned to go kept her silent.

Thoroughly puzzled by the shift in his mood at the mention of his family and his abrupt departure, she slowly went inside, settled down on her sofa, and stared thoughtfully into the gathering darkness. How could he claim to love her, yet not trust her with this secret, whatever it was? Mark seemed so secure, so self-assured. Goodness knows, he claimed to be absolutely certain about his feelings toward her. Yet he was obviously afraid of her reaction to what he might say about his own life. Why? What in his background could possibly be so terrible that he would consider it a threat to their relationship?

- 4 -

WHEN ERIN'S ALARM went off the next morning at the uncivilized hour of five, she was still exhausted from a night of confusing dreams, all of them centering around Mark Townsend. She felt as though she'd been tossed overboard and left to founder in a tumultuous sea. She had known the man for barely two days, and already she had the feeling she was going under for the third time. What really concerned her was that she couldn't think of a single soul who would toss her a lifeline. Her entire family thought she'd been wading in the shallows of romance for too long now. They'd be delighted to hear that she was in deeper emotional waters—even if they were way over her head.

She moaned and rolled over, wishing she could bury herself under the covers and stay hidden for the rest of the day. She peeked at the clock and sighed. No way. She had exactly one hour to pull herself together, straighten up her tiny apartment, and get to her call at a studio across town. She was scheduled to begin shooting a commercial at seven, and it was going to take Derrick an hour just to mask the dark circles she knew were under her eyes after her restless night.

She crawled out of bed and quickly flipped the sofa bed closed so it couldn't tempt her, tossed a row of colorful pillows across it, and tugged the coffee table back into place. After showering and brushing her teeth, she pulled on a bright-green leotard, added a pair of faded jeans, and completed the outfit with a bulky cardigan that fell nearly to her knees. Then she twisted her hair into a loose knot on top of her head, dumped her makeup into her oversized handbag, and raced down the stairs. Josh was parked at the curb, reading the sports page. He glanced up as she tapped on the window, then jumped into the back of the cab.

"You look terrible," he greeted her with a glance in the rearview mirror.

"Thanks. That was just the boost I needed this morning."

"What's the problem?"

"As if you didn't know."

"Did you have brunch with Mark Townsend yesterday?"

"How could I avoid it? You practically left a trail of breadcrumbs all the way to my doorstep."

"Hey, don't blame me. I didn't say a thing to him."

Erin regarded him closely, looking for signs of some male conspiracy of silence. She didn't see any. Puzzled, she muttered, "That's what *he* said."

"And you didn't believe him?"

"Well, how else could he have found me?"

"Erin, there are any number of ways a resourceful

man can go about tracking down a woman."

Resourceful. It was an appropriate word choice. Mark was, after all, a private investigator. No doubt, they were even more resourceful than your average bachelor on the run. Still, it was a bit disconcerting to know that he could discover things about her life so easily.

"He seemed like a nice guy," Josh interrupted her thoughts. He sounded disgustingly hopeful.

"He is a nice guy. . ."

"But?"

"Josh, how many times do I have to remind you that I am not looking for someone in my life?"

"You should be."

"Why?"

"You're an attractive, vital woman, Erin. And whether you'll admit it or not, you're lonely as hell. There's no excuse for it, either."

"I am not lonely," she snapped defensively.

"No, of course not," he said sarcastically, and Erin could see the quirk of his eyebrows in the mirror. "You have your aerobics class on Tuesday, your acting class on Wednesday, and what is it on Thursday? Ballet? Oh, and I shouldn't leave out Saturdays at the museum. I'm only surprised you haven't thrown in macramé and Chinese cooking."

"I took them last year."

"I rest my case."

Erin glared at him. "What's wrong with taking classes? I meet a lot of interesting people, and I need those classes if I'm ever going to grow as an actress."

"And how do you plan on growing as a human being? By talking to a cat?"

"I don't have a cat. It would kill my mouse."

Josh groaned. "That's not the point. You're shutting yourself off from life, kiddo. You have been ever since you split with Terry."

Fortunately, before he could continue his favorite lecture on the subject of not allowing her rotten ex-husband's behavior to color the rest of her life, they arrived at the studio.

"Thanks for the ride and the psychoanalysis," she told him with mock sweetness. "Other people pay eighty bucks an hour for the sort of advice I get from you in a fifteen-minute taxi ride."

"Maybe I should charge you," he quipped with a grin. "At those prices, you'd probably listen to me."

Inside the studio, Erin greeted Donald Wainwright, the director, waved at the crew, and went straight into a dressing room to have her makeup and hair done. While Derrick fussed over her, lecturing her on taking better care of herself, she tried to run through her lines. But Josh's words kept breaking into her dialogue. A part of her knew he was right, that sooner or later she was going to have to start taking chances again, but, as intrigued as she was beginning to be with Mark, it was still too soon.

Donald stuck his head in the door. "Ready, Erin?"

She smiled at him. This, at least, was something she understood, something she could handle. "Anytime you are."

"Then let's go. This should be a fairly routine shoot. If you're all doing your jobs, we'll be out of here early."

Five exhausting hours later, it appeared that everyone except Erin had his or her job down pat. She, on the other hand, had managed to fluff more lines than she had since her first performance in kindergarten.

"Blast it all, why can't I get this right?" she muttered

in disgust. "Sorry, Donald. Let's try it again."

She sank back down on her hands and knees to scrub a spotlessly white toilet bowl. She looked down at the rumpled red plaid blouse and wrinkled jeans provided by wardrobe.

"Donald, do you want to press these before we shoot again?"

"No. You look fine. We're trying to show how tiring the old methods are anyway. The outfit looks perfect for that," he said with a definite edge to his voice. Donald was one of the most easygoing directors Erin had ever worked for, but even his patience was beginning to wear thin. Erin winced.

So much for the glamorous life of an actress. At the rate she was going, she'd wind up with housemaid's knees, a backache, and a rotten reputation as an actress by the end of the shoot. With damp tendrils of hair clinging to her flushed face, she sighed and plunged a brush back into the toilet bowl, glanced toward Donald for her cue, and suddenly froze as she spotted Mark standing in the shadows at the back of the studio.

"Oh, my God," she muttered under her breath.

"Cut!" Donald snapped impatiently. "What is it now, babe?"

"Nothing," she replied weakly.

Mark grinned and waved. "Hi, princess."

Donald sighed heavily. "Do you want to take a break, Erin?"

"No," she said, glaring at Mark. "I definitely do not want to take a break."

"Then let's try this again . . . for the last time, I hope."

For some reason, Mark's flesh-and-blood presence seemed to galvanize Erin as effectively as his mere image had distracted her. Her powers of concentration returned, no doubt largely due to her determination to ignore the man who was watching her from the shadows. This time the lines flowed perfectly.

"Okay!" Donald shouted gleefully. "That's a wrap. I want everyone back here in exactly one hour. We'll finish up then."

He walked over to Erin, who was still sitting on the small section of tile floor. "I don't know what happened to you on that last take, sweetheart, but if you can keep it up this afternoon, we're going to have the sexiest toilet bowl cleanser commercial on the air."

Erin narrowed her eyes and asked suspiciously, "What are you talking about?"

"Sweetheart, you had a look on your face that could have lit up Manhattan. If we owe that to your friend back there, ask him to stick around."

"Terrific," Erin muttered. "First he tries to take over my personal life, and now he's taking over my career. The next thing I know Mark Townsend will be as essential to my well-being as vitamins."

As soon as Donald walked away, Mark strolled over to her, his face alight with impish delight. "You were wonderful, princess."

"Thanks," she said, grudgingly acknowledging the compliment. "But what are you doing here? How did you find me?"

"Aren't you glad to see me?"

"Do you really want an answer to that?"

"Of course."

"Then, no. Frankly, I am not glad to see you. Why are you here? Don't you have a job someplace?"

Ignoring her sarcastic tone and the fire in her eyes,

he gestured to the bathroom set, the bottle of cleanser, and her own untidy appearance. "I've come to take you away from all this," he said lightly.

Refusing to succumb to his teasing, Erin countered, "But this is my job. I don't want to be taken away from it."

"Lighten up, princess. I just stopped by to visit."

"I don't interrupt you at your job."

"Sure you do. I haven't been able to think about anything else all morning."

"That's different."

"How?"

"It just is," she responded desperately. "Dammit all, Mark, just because I don't sit behind a desk or stand in front of a classroom or something, it doesn't mean you can just come barging in here anytime you want. This may not be Shakespeare, but they pay me to work here. They don't pay me to sit around and chat."

"Lordy, you sound stuffy, princess. We're going to have to do something about that after we're married or you'll wind up with an ulcer. How much time do you have for lunch?"

"You are not listening to me. I don't have time for lunch." Her voice rose, infuriating her even more. The man was completely unnerving her, all the more so because, despite her sharp tone, she was unaccountably glad to see him. That he had gone out of his way to find her made her feel special again, desirable.

"I figured you'd say that," he commented complacently, sauntering to the back of the studio and returning with a bulging bag and a blanket.

"What's that?" she asked suspiciously.

He pulled out a bottle of wine, sandwiches, and fruit.

"Lunch for the busy actress." With a flourish he added a small bud vase with a single red rose. "And a flower for my true love."

Erin's pulse lurched erratically, then settled into high gear. She tried putting her hands on her hips defiantly and glaring at him, but it didn't do a bit of good. He was looking at her with such hope, such blasted good humor.

"Okay," she finally relented with a sigh and a hint of a smile. Lordy, the man was appealing. He knew exactly how to get to her, how to cut through her defenses. "I suppose it won't hurt to have lunch."

"Of course not," he said, spreading the blanket on the studio floor and sitting down cross-legged. "Have a croissant. Ham and cheese or sliced chicken?"

"Chicken."

"Appropriate choice," he taunted.

"Don't start on me, Mark."

He threw his hands up in a gesture of surrender that Erin didn't believe for a moment. Mark might be giving her a break for the next forty-five minutes or so, but she knew his campaign was far from over. Worse, she knew from the way her pulse had continued to race even after she'd stopped being mad at him that he was beginning to win. His unexpected appearance had made a rotten morning infinitely brighter. And his lighthearted banter during lunch left her weak from laughing. There was no sense of pressure, only that crazy sense of fun that beguiled her even as it worried her.

When the crew began drifting back into the studio, Mark gathered up the remnants of their picnic without a single hint from her. "I'm out of here. I've got work to do. I'll see you tonight."

Instantly the pressure was back.

"I won't be home," she said quickly, desperate to keep him from once more closing in too fast.

"Everyone has to come home sometime."

"It'll be very late," she said.

"I'll be waiting," he responded emphatically, putting his fingertips against her lips to silence her protest. The innocent contact sent a shiver racing along her spine. "Have a good afternoon."

Before she could say another word, before she could shout at him to leave her alone long enough to catch her breath, he was gone. She groaned.

"Damn. What am I supposed to do now?"

"Were you talking to me, Erin?"

"No, Donald. I was talking to myself. I seem to be doing that a lot lately."

"Could it possibly have anything to do with Sir Galahad there?"

"Why would you say that? I hardly know the man."

"That may be, but from what I saw, if he has anything to say about it, that's going to change faster than you can slip into your next costume."

Erin decided to ignore Donald's astute observation. "What are you doing for dinner tonight?" she asked instead.

"I have a date."

So did everyone else Erin could think of to call. She wound up eating alone in a neighborhood deli, lingering as long as she could over the bowl of chicken soup and salad she'd ordered. Eventually, though, she knew she'd have to go home. And, she was equally certain, Mark could be waiting on her doorstep. She was coming to realize that he was a man of his word. The realization should have pleased her, but instead it terrified her. His word included the promise that barely one week from now he was going to marry her.

When she finally walked into her building a few minutes after eight, true to his promise he was sitting on the steps waiting for her. A very solid wooden door was propped against the wall beside him. Erin couldn't help smiling.

"Other people bring flowers," she noted dryly.

"This seemed more practical."

"Don't tell me I'm converting you."

"Hardly. I just figured the way to your heart was more likely to be through your bathroom door, since you seem to like to hide in there."

"I do not hide in there!"

"What do you call it?"

"It's . . . it's . . ."

"I'm getting too close?" he guessed.

"Maybe," she admitted as they went inside.

Her answer seemed to satisfy him. He merely nodded and dropped the subject. "Give me a screwdriver, and I'll put this up for you," he said.

"You know where the screwdriver is," she said, sinking down on the sofa in exhaustion.

He regarded her skeptically. "Have you reset the mousetrap?" he asked cautiously.

Erin grinned and shook her head. "Don't tell me the hero has lost his sense of adventure."

"Nope. He's just learned his lesson."

While he worked on replacing the bathroom door, cheerfully humming off-key, Erin watched him in consternation. How could he possibly be so sure of what he wanted?

"Mark," she began at last, "tell me something seriously. What makes you think you're in love with me? You are a wonderfully crazy, impetuous man. I have a feeling you probably disappear and reappear like a rabbit in a magician's act. I'm traditional. I need order in my life. I have to know I can count on people. I have to think things through. They have to make sense. You can't make me over into your image."

"I like your image just fine," he offered suggestively.

"That's not what I meant."

He sighed. "I know it's not. Princess, I don't think love is something you can explain. It's just a feeling you get about someone."

"A purely physical feeling," she said dryly.

"That, too," he agreed. "But it's more than that. You're . . . I don't know how to phrase it any better . . . you're special. You care about things, about people. You make *me* feel special."

Erin blinked at him in surprise. That was exactly how he had been making her feel, but she'd had no idea she was having the same effect on him. And yet it was true. Mark was special. He had a uniquely endearing personality, and she had begun to see glimpses of his sensitivity. Certainly he wasn't afraid to take risks, and that confidence appealed to her. As long as the risks he took weren't too great, too dangerous, she clarified.

"But I'm so much more cautious than you are," she told him, still trying to pinpoint why she believed that no matter how strong the attraction, in the end they were totally mismatched.

His eyes twinkled as he looked over at her. "I don't think you give yourself enough credit. You can be impulsive. Just look at the way we met."

"That was my job," she reminded him. "I'm an actress. In my roles, yes, sometimes I'm kooky, too.

But in real life I take things seriously. You and I are very different people."

"I don't think so," he insisted stubbornly. "I think buried in that stuffy subconscious of yours is a wild, crazy lady yearning to be free. I even think you became an actress so you could indulge your kookier impulses."

Erin had never thought of it quite that way before. Perhaps from time to time she did want to escape from her own fear of instability, to simply have fun and still pay the bills. Although acting was hardly as stable as computer technology, it did permit that sort of compromise, if you knew how to minimize the risks. "Mark . . ."

He came and sat next to her, again placing a finger on her lips to silence her doubts. "Even if there's not a free spirit lurking in there, I don't think I could stop loving you. That's just something that is, princess. For better or for worse."

"Worse being the awful possibility that I'm not as loony as you and that I'll turn out to be utterly boring and predictable?" she said acerbically.

"How can anyone who scrubs toilets in front of a camera one day and dresses up in evening clothes to sell perfume another day be considered predictable?" he retorted.

Erin looked at him oddly. What did Mark know about her commercial for Jasmine Cosmetics? It wasn't even on the air yet. "Mark, how do you know about that?"

"About what?"

"The perfume commercial."

"Um," he began, looking distinctly guilty, "isn't it on the air?"

"No."

"Then I must have read about it."

"Where? I haven't seen anything."

"You probably just missed it. It must have been in one of those advertising trade papers."

"Why do I have the feeling there's something you're not telling me?"

"Like what? Princess, it's no big deal. The point I was trying to make was that you can have it all: the stability you need, plus the excitement. Having fun doesn't mean being irresponsible."

He pulled her into his arms then, kissing her slowly, his lips velvet fire against hers. Passion stirred deep inside Erin, a molten warmth that stole through her blood and made it sizzle. His hands on her shoulders burned through her blouse, branding her with his possession. Feelings that had been buried for years roared to life with undeniable urgency.

Erin tried to take a deep breath, desperately wanting to return to sanity, to the uncomplicated existence that was rapidly giving way to a tidal wave of unwanted sensations and emotions. She needed to cling to the calm a little longer. "Mark, no. Please."

Slowly, reluctantly, he released his hold on her, but a lingering flame lit his gray eyes, making them gleam. They were eyes that would captivate, eyes that spoke of excitement, enchantment, eyes that spoke of love. It was too much. Too soon. Erin forced herself to look away.

"Mark, we can't keep seeing each other like this."

"Princess, I know you're feeling crowded, that you'd rather hide from your feelings, but it's time to stop running."

She shook her head. "I can't."

"Yes, you can," he said firmly, then added more softly, "I have."

Before she could ask what he meant, he stood and walked out the door, leaving her to ponder through another night what had made Mark Townsend into the intriguing, contradictory, sensitive man who seemed to be turning her entire, predictable world topsy-turvy.

- 5 -

ELENA'S BODY SHOP rocked to a powerful beat, and Erin was happily jogging in place in time to the music. Perspiration streamed down her face as she tried to concentrate on keeping her breathing steady. Suddenly she heard a collective sigh from the members of her Tuesday-night aerobics class. Glancing into the wall-to-wall mirror in front of her, she saw three rows of sweaty, exhausted women—and one clean-cut man with wheat-blond hair, twinkling gray eyes, and a perfectly spotless running suit that looked as though it had never known a moment's exercise. Her head whipped around so fast, she wondered if she could sue him for whiplash.

Ignore him, she instructed herself firmly, rubbing a towel across her face. Ignore him and he will disappear. Close your eyes for fifteen seconds, open them, and he will be gone. She tried it. When she opened her eyes

57

again, he was working his way through the wide-eyed, smirking women to reach her.

"Hi, princess," he said cheerfully. "How's it going?"

"It *was* going just fine," she responded significantly.

"Aren't you glad to see me?"

The question was getting to be awfully familiar. Unfortunately, so was the answer. She was getting to be more and more glad to see him each time he popped up with his dazzling smile. She was also fighting those feelings like crazy.

"An astute man would know the answer to that," she responded dryly. "How did you find me, by the way? And how did you talk your way past the receptionist? Last I heard she was pretty good at detecting gender, and you definitely do not qualify for this class."

"Which do you want me to answer first?"

"Take your pick."

"Finding you was easy. I'm a private investigator, remember? We spend our lives finding people who don't want to be found."

"Don't you have some criminal you could concentrate on for the next few days?"

"Sorry. You're my main quarry. We have a wedding date to keep."

"Dear God!" she moaned, noticing the interested glances from her classmates. "Not that again."

"Surely you didn't think I was going to forget about it?"

"I suppose not. What about your gate-crashing skills? I suppose that has something to do with being a private investigator, too."

"Not exactly. I promised Alicia two tickets to the hottest show on Broadway."

One eyebrow shot up. "My, my. Alicia, is it? Not even Ms. Thomas?"

He winked at her. "Just trying to be friendly."

"Are you part of this theater package you've offered our intrepid receptionist?"

He shrugged, and his expressive face was far from innocent. In fact, he was beginning to look guilty as hell. "She may have gotten that idea," he admitted at last, adding quickly, "But I swear to you, I have no intention of going out with anyone but you between now and the wedding."

At her quizzical look, he amended, "Or ever again." He looked at her more closely. "By the way, are you sure this is good for you? Your face is all red."

"That's because I'm trying not to scream."

"Oh, princess," he said, his expression so woebegone that Erin promptly relented.

"Okay. I'm sorry. But if you're planning to stay here, you're going to have to do what the rest of us do," she informed him sternly.

He glanced around warily, then grinned that heart-tumbling smile that was beginning to melt her wall of defenses as though it had been constructed of nothing sturdier than ice. "You mean jump up and down? No problem."

Elena overheard the smug comment, winked at Erin, and put a new tape into the player. A song with a violent, dangerously fast beat throbbed through the room.

"Okay, you guys," the tiny woman shouted cheerfully. "Enough lazing around. Let's get with it. Get those legs up. I want to see your knees touch your chests when you jog. Now swing those arms over your head. Higher. Reach. Reach."

After the first minute, Erin glanced surreptitiously in Mark's direction. He was stripping off his warm-up suit. Underneath he had on gym shorts and a sweatshirt with the sleeves cut off. He looked incredibly fit—gorgeous, in fact.

"Careful, guy!" she warned with a grin. "There are passion-starved women in here who might not be able to control themselves if they glimpse too much of that incredible body."

"Are you one of them?" he inquired hopefully.

Erin's eyes drifted over the muscular arms that were becoming slick with perspiration, the well-toned legs with their haze of golden hairs, and found that her own breathing was a bit more ragged than she could blame on the exercise.

"Scared to answer, huh?"

"Save your breath, Mark," she warned him. "You're going to need it."

The two-and-a-half-minute song ended just then, but before the participants could catch their breath, another song had replaced it and Elena was urging them on again. Erin expected to see some signs of exhaustion or dismay on Mark's face by now, but he was breezing through their strenuous routine. She had to admit she was impressed. She also had to acknowledge that she'd picked the wrong way to get even with him for tracking her down yet again. If anything, he was in better shape than the majority of the women in the room who'd been taking the class for months.

When Elena finally called it quits, Mark snatched Erin's towel from her and sat down on one of the uncomfortable metal chairs that had been left in the room for those dauntless souls whose enthusiasm outdistanced their wind.

"Tired?" she asked hopefully.

"Not a bit," he said cheerfully. "That was fun. I could use a shower, though."

"Sorry. There's just one locker room, and at this hour it's for women only."

"Princess, if I take you out to dinner in this condition, we'll have to sit at separate tables."

"How about separate restaurants?" she taunted.

"Cute."

Erin relented. "I suppose you could use the showers after everyone else is finished."

"You're quite a sport."

"Not really. I'm just not a particular fan of Eau de Exercise."

"Are you sure?" he asked softly, a dangerous glint lighting his eyes. The look should have warned her, but it didn't. Suddenly, before she could anticipate what was on his mind, he was on his feet and pulling her into his arms. Gentle hands ran over her perspiration-slick shoulders and arms, creating an unbearably sensual tension that brought every nerve ending alive. Stunned by her body's instantaneous reaction, Erin lifted startled brown eyes to meet his teasing gaze.

"Personally, I've always found Eau de Exercise an intoxicating aphrodisiac," he whispered huskily, his lips brushing lightly down the side of her damp neck. "On you it's irresistible," he murmured as his kisses followed the curve of her throat until he reached the throbbing pulse that proved beyond any doubt that she was not immune to his caresses. Erin moaned softly and found her arms slipping around his waist to bring his muscular body into dangerously sizzling contact with the full length of hers.

Then his lips were on hers, hungrily claiming them,

urging them apart with a tongue that teased and taunted. Erin would never have believed that her already over-heated body could burn even more feverishly, but it did, this time from the inside out, as a slow warmth built into a raging fire. The hard evidence of his arousal excited her and terrified her at the same time. Through a haze of pure sensation, she realized that she wanted Mark, needed him in some elemental way that she tried to convince herself was tied only to physical desire. It had been so long, forever it seemed, since she had felt this way, her body yearning, craving for fulfillment and sensing that it was within her grasp. She moved against Mark, her hips instinctively undulating.

Suddenly he moaned, a husky growl that rumbled deep in his chest, and moved away from her.

"Princess, I have always wanted to make love in a mirrored room," he said shakily, "but not when fifty women are likely to wander through at any moment."

"Oh," she said softly, reluctantly slipping from his embrace as an embarrassed awareness of her surround-ings slowly returned.

"Oh, indeed!" He seemed to sense her confusion. "I don't suppose you'd consider giving me a raincheck for later on at your place?"

Erin shook her head as though to clear it. The gesture had no effect on her pounding heart, but sanity did seem to be returning bit by bit. "Dinner," she said vaguely, avoiding his question as though it hadn't registered . . . or had registered all too clearly and was something she preferred not to deal with.

Mark chuckled. "Not exactly the answer I was after, but it'll do for starters. Go take your shower."

By the time Erin had showered and waited for Mark to use the cleared-out locker room, her reeling thoughts were under better control. Her physical attraction to Mark had not come as a complete surprise to her, but the depth of it had rocked her to her very core. She knew herself well enough to know that such a reaction had to do with more than simple lust. He was beginning to reach her on some other level. She was starting to trust him, to be thoroughly enchanted by him, and she didn't have the vaguest idea why she was allowing it to happen. Those few minutes in his arms had proved one thing to her, though: She either had to allow this relationship to take its natural course, whatever it might be, or run for her life. The former still terrified her, but the latter left her feeling empty and lonely. She sighed. Maybe it was a decision she wouldn't have to make tonight, though she realized she was only delaying the inevitable. How long could you put off making a decision about a man who intended to marry you in a week?

"Ready, princess?"

Erin took a deep, steadying breath and smiled. "Ready. Where are we going?"

"I'm in the mood for a giant-sized pizza with extra cheese, pepperoni, onions, green peppers, and sausage."

Erin's eyes widened. "You've got to be kidding."

"All that exercise worked up my appetite. I suppose you'd prefer a salad and a side order of bean sprouts?"

"Well . . ." she admitted.

"Forget it. That's not healthy. You'll starve to death."

"I haven't so far."

"When was the last time you had a big, thick, gooey slice of pizza with everything on it?"

"My senior year in college."

Mark shook his head sorrowfully. "You've obviously been seriously deprived these last few years. Don't worry, though. I'm going to fix you right up."

"Are you going to sit up with me all night, when I have heartburn?"

"I thought you'd never ask," he teased with a soft gleam in his eyes.

When they reached a small Italian restaurant a few blocks away, Erin took a deep breath of the air, which was fragrant with garlic, tomato sauce, and spices. It did smell heavenly, bringing back blissful memories of late-night feasts in her college dorm.

"We'll take your biggest pizza with everything except anchovies," Mark told the waitress. He glanced at Erin. "Beer?"

"Diet soda."

"You're incorrigible."

"I have to take the calories out of something."

"Okay. One beer. One diet cola." When the waitress had left, he gazed at Erin and asked, "So. How was your day? Did you scrub any more toilet bowls?"

"Nope. I just went on rounds."

"Meaning?"

"I lugged my portfolio from one ad agency to another to check out possible parts my agent had lined up."

"Anything look promising?"

Erin looked at him skeptically. Terry had never cared about her career. Whenever she'd wanted to tell him about an exciting opportunity, he'd either tuned out or not even been there in the first place. "Do you really care about this?"

"I care about everything you do," he said adamantly.

Erin shrugged and began talking, her excitement mounting. "Okay. Yes. One job did look promising. It's not a commercial, though. It's on one of the soaps. I met with the casting director. They're looking for someone to come into town and stir up the tranquil waters."

To her chagrin, Mark chuckled. "You?"

"Why are you laughing?"

"Because you look much too sweet and innocent to play one of those vicious, sexy troublemakers."

"Thanks a lot," she replied sarcastically.

"I meant it as a compliment."

"I'm an actress. I should be able to play any part."

"Okay. Sorry," he said contritely, still struggling to hide a grin. "What did they say?"

"They want me to come back next week for an audition. I have a couple of scenes to learn, and then they'll try me out with the leading man."

"You mean love scenes?"

"One of them is."

"Need any help rehearsing?" he inquired hopefully. "I'd be glad to help out."

"I'll just bet you would."

"Good," he said, interpreting her comment as assent. "I can hardly wait."

"Mark," she protested just as the waitress arrived with their drinks and a pizza that virtually covered the tabletop.

"Later, princess. We have serious work ahead of us."

"You don't actually think we can eat this entire thing, do you?" Erin asked, her stomach already protesting.

"Every bite," he replied. "And I expect you to do your part."

For several minutes they were too busy with the gooey wedges of pizza to talk, but when Erin had finished two pieces, she groaned and pushed the platter toward Mark. "That's it. No more."

"Erin, there's more than half a pizza left. You can't stop now."

"Watch me," she replied, sitting back and taking a

sip of her diet cola. She studied Mark as he ate, wondering again just what made him tick. She had sensed so many contradictions in him, so many facets. He was like a sparkling diamond that revealed something different with each new examination. As an actress, she liked to study human nature in general, always in search of something that might add to a later performance. As a woman, she was growing increasingly curious about the very specific man seated across from her.

"Mark, why did you decide to become a private investigator?"

A shadow crossed his gray eyes, momentarily turning them dark and stormy, and Erin could feel him withdrawing from her. "You don't start with the easy ones, do you?" he said quietly.

Erin was puzzled by the response. What was so difficult about explaining a career choice? And, yet, it was clear that he found the subject disconcerting. "If you'd rather not talk about it . . ."

"No. It's okay. I'm just not sure where to begin."

He put down the slice of pizza he'd been holding and took a deep swallow of beer.

"Is anyone in your family a private investigator?" Erin prodded.

Mark clearly found the suggestion amusing. "Hardly. My family is very staid, very traditional. My father runs Townsend Industries, a conglomerate that owns everything from computer companies to oil fields."

"And I'll bet he expected you to go into the family business," Erin guessed. She could only imagine the reaction of a man like that to his son's decision to become a private investigator instead.

"You've got it," Mark confirmed. "He was not happy

about what he described as my ridiculous, adolescent rebellion."

Erin grinned at that description. Mark had struck her as stubborn, not rebellious. She'd also envisioned him as the attractive and charming class clown, who had all of the girls madly in love with him. "Is that what it was? An adolescent rebellion?"

Mark shook his head. "No. Not at all. Actually, it was a futile attempt at a compromise. I wanted to be a cop. You should have heard him when I suggested that one."

"I can imagine." Erin studied him thoughtfully, fascinated at the information he had let slip about his uneasy relationship with his father. "Were you just being stubborn, or was there some reason you wanted to be a policeman? It does seem like an odd choice for someone from your world."

His gray eyes hardened to the color of slate. "My world?" he said with unexpected bitterness. "There's nothing so exclusive about my world. It's not immune to crime."

The depth of his anger startled her, and she looked at him in bewilderment. There were obviously emotions boiling just below the surface here that she didn't understand at all. Mark had seemed so carefree, so lighthearted in the short time she'd known him. But apparently there were painful parts of his past that he kept closely guarded, buried under a facade of easygoing humor.

"What is it you're not saying?" she probed.

He shook his head. "Nothing," he insisted. "We'll talk about it another time."

Erin was reluctant to let the subject drop. She had a

feeling it was important, too important to ignore, if she were ever to really know Mark. And her need to know him was growing day by day. "Please, Mark."

"No, princess." He gave her a wobbly, conciliatory smile that made her heart flip over. "Why don't we talk about something else? How about our wedding?" he suggested lightly. "We don't have a lot of time left to plan."

It was the last topic Erin had expected him to bring up in his present mood, and it was certainly the last thing she wanted to discuss. "Mark, there is not going to be any wedding," she retorted emphatically. "Not as long as you won't talk about things that are important."

"I think our wedding is pretty important," he countered. "I've been thinking about having it in a castle, someplace suitable for a princess. What do you think?"

"I think you're not listening to me. No castle. No wedding."

The zany, whimsical Mark was suddenly back, and Erin wasn't sure whether to welcome him or strangle him. "Maybe you're right," he conceded. "A castle probably would be damp, and they're awfully hard to come by in New York City, anyway. What about the Staten Island Ferry? With any luck it would be a gorgeous, sunny day with all of Manhattan glittering in the background."

"Are you completely off your rocker? Weddings are supposed to take place in churches, while the organ plays in the background and the bride marches down the aisle in a stunning gown with a bouquet of orchids and baby's breath. A crummy old boat in the middle of an equally crummy river is not my idea of romantic."

Mark grinned at her. "Okay," he said agreeably, obviously sensing some sort of victory Erin hadn't intended at all. "If that's what you want, a church it is. When?"

"Wait a minute! I have not agreed to any wedding."

"Are you sure? I could have sworn I just heard you say yes."

"No, you just heard me discuss, in a perfectly theoretical manner, what weddings are supposed to be like. I said nothing at all about yours and mine."

"Then we are having a wedding," he said triumphantly.

"No, dammit. I didn't say that either."

"Princess, you're going to have to get a grip on yourself. You're beginning to ramble."

Erin moaned. "Before you're through, I'm going to be just as crazy as you are."

"Exactly," Mark said, looking disgustingly satisfied with himself. "More pizza?"

"You are . . ." An appropriate word escaped her.

"Wonderful?" he suggested.

"I was thinking more along the lines of impossible."

"Oh, princess," he said softly, giving her a dazzling smile, "together we can make anything possible."

- 6 -

LATE THE NEXT afternoon, when Erin came out of her
acting class, a steady rain was pouring from a lead-gray
sky. She moaned as she looked at the bumper to bumper
traffic. She would never get a cab in this downpour. She
was firmly convinced every taxi driver in New York
decided to take a coffee break the minute the first drop
of rain fell.

Struggling against the wind with her oversized
umbrella, she was just about to dart across the street to
the bus stop when Josh's taxi zigzagged through the
traffic and pulled up in front of her.

"Are you a mindreader?" she said gratefully as she
climbed into the backseat and shook the water off her
striped umbrella before closing it and pulling it inside.
"What on earth would I do without you?"

"Catch pneumonia probably," he said matter-of-factly as he inched back into the snarled traffic.

"You're probably right. How's Maureen?"

"Fine. But the kids are all just getting over colds." He turned around and made a face. "God, they're impossible when they're sick. They all think they're supposed to get orange juice and ice cream on command."

"That's Maureen's doing."

"Of course it is, but she's not the one who gets sent out at nine at night to pick up a half-gallon of strawberry swirl."

"You know you love it."

"Heck no, I like chocolate marshmallow."

Erin laughed. "That is not what I meant, Josh Lawrence, and you know it. You love being needed by those little warriors of yours."

He looked back at her and smiled. "You think so? You try taking care of them sometime." His dark eyes took on a hopeful gleam. "Like maybe tomorrow night."

"So you and Maureen can have a romantic night alone?" Erin teased. "Do you want me to bring them into Manhattan to my place?"

"Your place is barely big enough for you, much less those three hellions. Why don't we trade? You stay out at our house, and Maureen and I can take a trip down memory lane and recall what it was like to have a night on the town, to say nothing of some peace and privacy."

"My pipes clank," Erin warned. "And Mrs. Bates listens to every creak of my bedsprings. You'll ruin my reputation."

"That's a small price to pay for your sister's sanity . . . to say nothing of the future of our marriage," Josh retorted. "Is it a deal?"

Erin appeared to give the matter grave consideration. "Erin, please," Josh begged.

"Of course, you idiot. I'd love to see the kids."

"You don't have other plans?"

She caught his innocently blank expression, a look he had clearly worked hard to achieve. "Why would you ask that?" she said suspiciously.

"I was under the impression that your friend Mark was keeping you very busy these days."

Erin sighed, wondering if they could possibly manage an entire conversation without that man's name surfacing.

"So it seems," she admitted. "But that doesn't mean I'm giving up the rest of my life to accommodate him. I'll be over at six," she said decisively. "Tell the kids I'll take them out for pizza."

Josh regarded her quizzically. "I thought you'd sworn off the stuff."

"I seem to have rediscovered my old craving," she admitted.

"Oh? To what . . . or whom . . . do we owe that?" His tone was entirely too gleeful.

"Shut up and pay attention to your driving, Josh. You've already missed the turn."

"No, I haven't."

"Josh Lawrence, I have lived in Manhattan for some time now. I think I know how to find my way home."

"But you're not going home."

Erin was struck by an increasingly familiar sinking sensation in the pit of her stomach. "I'm not? Please tell me this little detour does not have anything to do with Mark."

"Bingo."

"Not again," she protested. "Josh, this is kidnapping."

"No, it's not. You got into the cab willingly."

"I got into the cab expecting to go home. Where are you taking me?"

He shrugged. "Some swanky address on Madison Avenue."

"I don't suppose Mark mentioned why I'm meeting him there?"

"Not a word."

"Has it occurred to you that you are conspiring with the enemy?"

"Hey, he's not my enemy. I like the guy."

Erin felt like screaming, but instead she admitted softly, "I like him, too." She wasn't sure which startled her more: this sudden awareness of her growing attachment to Mark or her confession of it.

"Oh, really!" Josh's surprise was clearly feigned.

She glared at him. Confession had obviously been a lousy idea. "Don't try to make anything out of that."

"What's to make out of it? The man is attractive, intelligent, and obviously crazy about you. You'd have to be nuts not to like him."

"Don't you think you're being just a little bit quick to accept him? You don't know Mark."

"I know a guy who's sincere and honest when I see one. You hang out in enough locker rooms, you learn a lot about men. Mark Townsend has character, kiddo. You're a fool if you can't see that."

Erin regarded him oddly. "It sounds as if you've talked to him more than I realized."

"We've talked a couple of times. Had a few beers. No big deal."

"It is a big deal. He's been snooping around behind my back."

"I'd hardly call having a drink with your brother-in-law snooping around."

"Okay, maybe you're right," she admitted, then eyed Josh closely. "Maybe he's just trying to line up allies. It sounds as though he's succeeding. Has he gotten to Maureen yet?"

Josh grinned and chuckled. "Not yet, but she's climbing the walls. You know how your sister is when she starts feeling left out. Don't be surprised if she invites him over herself so she can get to know the man her little sister is going to marry."

"Marry? Not you, too!" Erin squealed. "Aren't you just slightly overanxious?"

"Mark said something about next week."

"He what?"

"You mean you haven't agreed to marry him?"

"Good Lord, Josh, I just met the man!"

"You said you liked him."

"I like small children and puppies, but that doesn't mean I want to take them into my home for the rest of my life."

"I think this is different."

"Damn right, it's different," she grumbled. "Mark Townsend is entirely too sure of himself. He's pushing, and I don't like to be pushed. Just look—"

"—what happened with Terry," he finished for her. "We all know in endless, painful detail what happened with Terry, but that doesn't mean that every man on the face of the earth is a louse. I'm not," he added with a smirk.

"Don't flatter yourself," Erin retorted. "The last few days have shown a few chinks in your sense of loyalty."

He pulled to the curb in front of a small but exclusive art gallery. "I think the jury's still out on that one, kiddo. Run along and see what Romeo has up his sleeve for tonight."

"I don't suppose I could convince you to turn this battle-worn taxi around and take me home so I could snuggle up with a good book?"

"Afraid not. I have to get home with the orange juice."

"Thanks, traitor," Erin sniped as she slipped out of the car, put up her umbrella, and ran to the gallery door. "Why do I have this feeling I've been thrown to the wolves again?" she muttered to no one in particular.

Inside the stark gallery with its jutting white walls that created a series of display alcoves, she gave her umbrella and jacket to a girl in jeans and a T-shirt with the face of a rock star emblazoned across the front. At least she wasn't underdressed in her leotard and wrap-around skirt, she thought as she scanned the crowd in search of Mark. Her traitorous heart lurched as she finally spotted him hidden in a back alcove, deep in conversation with a thin, dark-haired, dark-eyed man. As she was working her way toward them, Mark looked up, his eyes suddenly sparkling with pleasure. Responding to the warmth of his gaze, her blasted heart tumbled over again and did a couple of joyful flip-flops of its own.

At the same time, Mark's companion looked her over thoroughly, then nodded approvingly, dispelling her momentary pleasure. Erin felt as though she'd just been inspected and approved like some piece of USDA beef. She glowered at the two of them. Mark, obviously sensing that this was not the ideal time to introduce her to his friend, quickly shook the man's hand and came to meet her. He brushed a tantalizing, featherlight kiss across her lips.

"Hi. I'm glad you could make it."

He actually sounded as though she'd had a choice. "Was there any doubt?" she inquired sweetly. She shook her head in exasperation. "Haven't you ever heard of calling and asking for a date? It's a quaint old tradition, but one I find very effective."

"That takes too long."

"A phone call takes two minutes. Maybe three, if you give me a chance to think about my answer. You must have spent at least that long convincing Josh to deliver me to your doorstep."

"No. He's not nearly as stubborn as you are."

Erin glared at him, which had absolutely no effect. He was watching her with that amused quirk to his lips and those silver-gray eyes that caressed and cherished. It was a look that could have vanquished an entire roomful of staunch equal-rights proponents. Even with every one of her defenses in place, she wouldn't stand a chance, and her defenses were toppling over like rows of toy soldiers.

"Now that I'm here, would you like to tell me what this is all about?"

"I thought you might be interested in the exhibit. A friend of mine did it."

"The soulful one who looks as though he hasn't eaten in a month?"

"That's Jean-Pierre, all right. He's a sculptor. Come on and I'll show you his work."

They approached a display of twisted pieces of metal, chunks of rock, and what looked like the insides of a very large clock. Erin surveyed it carefully from every angle. Finally, her brown eyes twinkling wickedly, she asked, "Are you sure you've brought me to an art gallery and not a spare parts department?"

"Don't be rude," Mark chided her lightly. "It doesn't become the creative artist in you."

Her eyebrows rose questioningly. "Don't tell me you actually like this stuff."

Mark's expression wavered. "Well..." He seemed torn between honesty and his sense of loyalty.

"Admit it. You hate it, too."

"Okay. So I don't understand it," he confessed. "That doesn't mean it's not the work of a genius."

"According to whom?"

"Some critic I overheard gushing eloquently a minute ago."

"And you believed him?"

"I figure he probably knows more about this type of stuff than I do."

"Surely you've seen Jean-Pierre's work before."

"Yes."

"Did you think it was the work of a genius then?"

"Not really."

"Then why did you come tonight? Wasn't once enough to express your loyalty?"

"I came for Jean-Pierre's sake," he explained simply. "He needs protection."

"I can see why."

"You're a real wise guy, princess. I'm serious. He's had some problems lately with thieves and vandals. I promised to keep an eye on things for him."

"I thought you only dealt with people who stole secrets or paper clips."

"Occasionally I do odd jobs for my friends when they're in trouble."

Erin's heart seemed to screech to a stop. Trouble

usually went hand in hand with danger. "Do they get in trouble often?" she asked hesitantly, concerned about the panicky reaction she was having. It was a sign she was becoming involved. Much too involved.

"Not really."

"I think I liked it better when I thought of you tracking down some guy in a white shirt and striped tie who was hell-bent on using up the supply of Xerox paper for his own devious purposes."

"Most of the time that's exactly what I do."

"Thank God," she muttered fervently. Gazing at him curiously, she asked, "Do you actually think these vandals are likely to walk into this exhibit and start destroying Jean-Pierre's sculpture in front of two hundred people?"

"Probably not, but I promised him I'd be here, just in case."

Erin studied Mark thoughtfully. "I seem to be torn between two questions."

"Ask away."

"Exactly how are you planning to deal with these guys if they do show up?"

He shook his head. "It's probably better if we don't talk about that."

"You have a gun, don't you?" Her voice rose in fascinated horror.

A hand closed firmly over her mouth as Mark dragged her into a secluded corner before she could alert the entire room. "Erin, please!"

"But I hate guns!"

"I'm not wild about them, either, but they are an effective deterrent against a certain element of the population."

"Couldn't you just call the police?"

"They have guns, too."

"They're supposed to."

"I have a license for mine, too."

"That's different."

"Why?"

"You could be killed."

He sighed heavily. "Princess, I am not going to be killed. I seriously doubt if these guys who've been threatening Jean-Pierre will come anywhere near this place with all these witnesses standing around. Now, forget about it," he ordered firmly. "What was your other question?"

She swallowed nervously and tried to ignore the fact that a very deadly metallic weapon was tucked somewhere on Mark's person. "My other question?" she repeated blankly.

"You said you had two."

That seemed like a very long time ago. "Oh. Yes." She glanced around the room and stood on tiptoe to whisper in Mark's ear. "Why do you suppose all these people are really here? Surely even in New York this many people can't have such terrible taste."

A soft chuckle began in Mark's chest and finally erupted into a roar of laughter. "Oh, princess. You are too much."

"I'm serious," she told him indignantly.

Mark tried to assume a serious expression, though his lips were still twitching. He leaned over and whispered conspiratorially, "Haven't you noticed they're serving wine and hors d'oeuvres? Anytime you bring out free food, starving artists will flock to it like a swarm of ants."

"Very funny. Does anyone actually buy Jean-Pierre's work?"

"As of matter of fact, he just sold that piece you were making fun of."

"You're kidding!"

"Nope."

"For how much?"

"I think he said something about twenty-five thousand dollars."

Erin's eyes widened. "No," she said incredulously. "You must have misunderstood."

"Are you beginning to understand why he worries about thieves and vandals?"

Erin gave Mark an impish grin. "If you ask me, Jean-Pierre's the thief."

Just then a low, musical voice inquired, "Who is a thief, *ma chérie?*"

Erin swallowed guiltily and turned to face the dark, laughter-filled eyes of Jean-Pierre. She waited for Mark to extricate her from the awkward moment, but he seemed to find her discomfort amusing.

"Mark and I were just discussing your problems," she said at last, wishing she could think of some subtle way to let Mark know *his* problems were just beginning. The rat had obviously seen Jean-Pierre approach and had done nothing to warn her. "Is there anyone here tonight that you suspect?"

Jean-Pierre's expression suddenly sobered. "As a matter of fact, that is why I intruded. *Mon ami,*" he said quietly to Mark, "I have noticed a rather suspicious-looking gentleman who was not invited lingering near one of the pieces. I wonder if you could approach and learn who he is?"

"Of course. Just point him out."

"You will excuse us, mademoiselle?"

Erin wanted to refuse, to tell Mark to stay right

where he was, but she knew he'd only ignore her and make her request seem faint-hearted and foolish. "Certainly," she said, but she had to force the word past stiff lips.

Mark squeezed her hand. "I'll be back in a minute. Wander around and enjoy the exhibit."

"You bet," she responded tartly, watching him walk away and experiencing a strange feeling of dread. She tried to tell herself she was being ridiculous. This was not *Magnum, P.I.* or *Simon & Simon*. How much danger could Mark be in at a crowded art opening? The whole problem probably only existed in Jean-Pierre's imagination anyway. Eccentric artists were prone to outrageous fantasies, weren't they?

Just then she heard a collective gasp and a heavy thud. A woman's scream ripped through the babble of conversation, and the gallery went suddenly silent. Erin's heart slammed against her ribs, and she held her breath as she rushed from an alcove into the main room. She could see a man lying on the floor surrounded by people. Only his jeans-clad legs were visible from her perspective, and her pulse skipped erratically as she inched her way toward those legs, never taking her terrified eyes off them.

"It's not Mark," she murmured over and over again as she approached. "Please, God. It can't be Mark."

As she slipped through to the inner circle, she saw Jean-Pierre on the floor, Mark kneeling at his side. Feeling suddenly weak with relief, she offered a silent prayer of thanks as she knelt beside him.

"Is he okay?" she asked, her voice filled with concern even as her eyes radiated her joy at discovering that it was not Mark lying on that cold, hard floor. "Do we need an ambulance?"

"No," Mark said, his gaze capturing hers and holding it as if he could read her thoughts and knew, even more than she did, what they meant. "He'll come around in a minute. The guy just popped him in the jaw."

"Did you find out who he was and why he was here?"

Mark grinned ruefully. "No. I'm afraid he didn't wait around for introductions. He just promised to come back."

"What a pleasant idea."

"I thought so, too," he said as Jean-Pierre groaned and blinked.

"Mon Dieu," he moaned, rubbing his jaw. "I did not even see it coming."

"You were too busy making sure he kept his hands off your precious sculpture."

"He did not harm it?" Jean-Pierre asked anxiously.

"No," Mark reassured him. "As soon as he saw that you were down for the count, he slipped through the crowd and disappeared. I'm sorry, pal."

"Sorry about what?"

"I should have gone after him, but I was worried about you."

Jean-Pierre gave him a lopsided, painful grin as he got to his feet. "Do not fret, *mon ami*. I have the feeling you will have another chance at this one. He seems to be the persistent type."

Erin suddenly shuddered. Mark's arms were instantly around her, and his expression was filled with concern. "Hey, are you okay?"

"For a minute there I was just imagining what might have happened."

"Well, it didn't, so don't worry about it. I think you'd better go on home, though."

"What about you?"

"I'm staying here tonight. I have a feeling Jean-Pierre is right. Our friend may very well come back, and I think he should find a welcoming committee."

"Do you have to be on it?" Erin asked, but she already knew the answer. Mark was not about to let down his friend. She shook her head. "Never mind. Don't answer that. If you're staying, then I'm staying, too."

"No, you're not," he replied firmly.

"I am," she said stoutly even as he was guiding her toward the front door, picking up her jacket and umbrella, and hailing a cab. "Mark, you can't make me leave."

He grinned at her. "A couple of days ago you didn't think I could make you go anyplace you didn't want to go."

"You still can't."

"Did you want to come here tonight?" he inquired softly, brushing a kiss across her lips. "Tell the truth."

"No," she said, sighing as his lips reclaimed hers in a powerful, overwhelming assault that drained her energy yet left her feeling strangely exhilarated. "Yes."

Gray eyes twinkled down at her like silvery stars. "Which is it?"

"I don't know anymore."

"Go home and think about it, princess."

- 7 -

THE NEXT AFTERNOON as Erin rode the subway to her
sister's, she was grateful that Josh had suggested this
evening of babysitting. Not only did she love spending
time with her rambunctious nephews, but it was also
going to give her a perfect opportunity to do as Mark
had suggested: think about what was really happening
between the two of them. Over the last two days especially, her feelings toward him had begun to change, to
shift inexorably away from defensiveness to an honest
admission of the exciting, nerve-tingling responsiveness
he had aroused in her from the moment they met.

Even more than that, last night during those few
awful moments of uncertainty at Jean-Pierre's exhibit,
she had found herself in the unexpected position of feeling fiercely protective toward him. The feeling had
remained with her today as she'd repeatedly caught herself worrying about whether he'd come to any harm

after he had sent her away from the party. Such worrying was a sure sign that Mark was inching his way into her affections.

She had also been impressed by his determined loyalty to Jean-Pierre, even at the risk of his own safety. That, combined with his efforts to downplay that risk for her peace of mind, told her quite a lot about the type of man he was. She was beginning to believe that he was not irresponsible and undependable as Terry had been, that if he could be counted on to be there for his friends, he would surely be there for her, the woman he claimed to love.

Erin sighed. To be perfectly truthful, even without the sudden onset of concern for his safety and the slow realization of the true depth of his character, she had begun to realize that Mark was bringing something warm and special into her life, something she wasn't at all sure she was ready for . . . a reawakening of her emotions and her senses. He was also restoring her sense of fun, her ability to live for the moment occasionally, instead of always looking toward the future and the consequences of every tiny action.

She knew this growth she was experiencing was too precious for her to allow it to slip away. And, yet, coming as suddenly as it had, it scared the daylights out of her, made her want to run and hide. And that's just what she was doing tonight: hiding in order to buy herself some time and space to think.

Bracing herself against the brisk October wind, she hurried down the street toward Maureen's, a colorful swirl of fall leaves crunching under her feet. The row of brownstones, which were slowly being restored to create a middle-class neighborhood out of what had once seemed destined to become a slum, appealed to her artistic sense. The bright, beckoning lights on Maureen's porch and in the windows also drew her, hinting at the warmth and undemanding love she knew she would find inside. She ran up the steps, and even before she could ring the bell, the door flew open and three chattering whirlwinds captured her in chubby arms.

"Aunt Erin, guess what I did in school today!"

"Aunt Erin, are you going to stay with us all night? Will you tell us ghost stories?"

"Aunt Erin, Jeb threwed me on the floor and sat on my stomach. It hurt."

The last, choked out with tears, came from Todd, the baby of the family, who was a constant source of irritation to his roughhousing older brothers. He also provided them with an ideal target for their tormenting, though he was rapidly learning to stand up for himself.

"Hey, guys, one at a time. Let me get in the door and catch my breath," she said, affectionately tousling Todd's hair, which was the Matthews' dark brown whirled into a halo of curls, thanks to Josh. It was an enviable combination, she thought once again as she took off her jacket and hung it up. She bent down to gaze into Todd's tear-filled eyes. "You okay, pal?"

He sniffled and nodded, raising his arms to be picked up. Erin hefted him into her arms, tickling him until giggles replaced the tears.

"Aunt Erin, guess who's here?" Jeb said, wincing as Robby poked him sharply in the ribs.

"Shut up, dummy. We're not supposed to tell."

"Is Grandma here?" Erin asked hopefully. She hadn't seen her mother in a couple of weeks, and she could use a good, old-fashioned mother-daughter chat about now.

"No," Robby said, clearly disgusted by his brother's

big mouth. But apparently deciding that as long as the secret was spoiled, he might as well get in on the act of revealing it all, he added, "It's some guy Dad says you're going to marry."

"What?" Her voice rose in a dismayed shriek, and if Todd hadn't been clinging to her neck, she would have yanked her jacket off the coatrack and put it right back on. So much for her safe space. "Maureen!"

Her sister came flying down the stairs in her bathrobe, her shoulder-length brown hair still wet, her expression harried. She gave Erin a hug and a kiss on the cheek as she plucked Todd from Erin's arms and sent the boys into the den to watch TV. "Hi, Sis. That sounded like a distress call. What's wrong?"

"Tell me that Mark Townsend is not sitting in your living room."

Maureen guiltily avoided her gaze. "Well . . ."

"He's here, isn't he?"

"He's not in the living room," Maureen offered.

"Maureen!"

"Actually, he's down in the basement with Josh. They're playing with the furnace. It's on the fritz again."

"Couldn't you have called a repairman?"

Maureen grinned at her. "I really don't think that's why he came over."

Erin groaned. "Of course not."

"I like him, Sis. I think he's just right for you."

"So, he's bought your vote, too."

"Don't be silly. Josh has told me all about him, and what he didn't say I could see for myself."

"Are you sure you're not just eager to marry me off to the first eligible male in sight?"

"Of course not."

"Then why is he here?"

"To see you, dummy. To get to know your family."

"I suppose it was too much to hope that he would wait for an invitation," Erin grumbled. "Yes, indeed. He has to go and invade my private family territory. I thought at least over here I could have some time to myself."

"To do what? Try and talk yourself out of a relationship with him? Has it occurred to you that if the man has you this rattled, he might be worth hanging on to? I can't recall anyone else who's gotten to you this way."

"Don't be ridiculous. The only reason Mark has me rattled is because he keeps turning up like the proverbial bad penny. I don't seem to be able to take a step without him shadowing me. I know he's a private investigator, but I wish to hell he'd get off my case."

"You don't really mean that."

"Oh, yes, I do."

"Well, I don't think he's going to do that," Maureen replied calmly. "If the conversation I had with him earlier is any indication, he seems to be in love with you."

"That's crazy, Maureen. We've known each other less than a week."

"So, it was love at first sight."

"That only happens in the movies."

"No, honey, sometimes it happens in real life, too, if you open yourself up to the possibility. You've been hiding from life for far too long. Just for once why don't you go for it?"

"You sound like a beer commercial."

"That may be," she admitted, patting Erin's cheek. "But I'm giving you good advice, little sister. Listen to it."

Erin sighed and gazed at Maureen. "I'm scared," she confessed at last.

"Of what, for heaven's sake?"

"I'm afraid I'll fall in love, too, and then I'll find out it really is just a fantasy, just like Terry."

Maureen gave her a hug. "Honey, even from what little I've seen of him, Mark Townsend is no Terry. Deep inside I think you already know that. And you're not the same person you were six years ago, either. You're stronger, more sure of yourself. You're capable of making better choices now. As for the rest, you won't know until you try, will you?"

"Try what? Hi, princess."

Erin turned toward the sound of Mark's voice, her indignation at his blatant invasion of yet more of her space suddenly overshadowed by her need to see that he was all in one very desirable piece. "You're okay?" It was definitely more a question than a statement. Anxious eyes roved over him from head to toe, looking for signs of damage.

He grinned at her. "Of course I'm okay. Heroes always stick around for happy endings."

"Don't be smug," she chided him. "That fellow last night didn't seem too concerned about your heroic credentials. Did he come back?"

"What guy?" Maureen's curiosity was immediately aroused. She was looking back and forth between the two of them, apparently sensing that the tension had to do with more than Mark's unexpected appearance. "What are you two talking about?"

"It's nothing to worry about, hon," Josh interceded quickly. "Get your fanny upstairs and finish getting dressed before these two find out what they've gotten themselves into and decide to abandon us."

"Josh, I want to know what guy," Maureen repeated stubbornly.

Erin knew her sister well enough to know that she was not going to be satisfied by her husband's evasive answers. She sighed and said in the most matter-of-fact tone she could manage, "A friend of Mark's had some trouble with a thief last night, that's all. As you can see, everything's just fine."

Maureen studied her carefully. "You're sure? I'm not leaving this house if there's going to be trouble."

"The only trouble is going to be what happens if you don't get dressed in the next five minutes," Josh countered. "Now, move it, hot stuff. We have a date."

Erin chuckled as Maureen blushed at the blatantly suggestive look in Josh's eyes. Despite her apparent embarrassment, Maureen's hips swayed provocatively as she climbed the stairs. Erin had a feeling if Maureen kept that up, she just might wind up with a niece to go with those three boisterous boys in the other room.

A half hour later, amid many hugs and kisses, Maureen and Josh took off for the city, leaving Mark and Erin alone with the kids.

"Are we going out for pizza, Aunt Erin? Daddy said you promised."

Erin avoided Mark's triumphant gaze. "Wouldn't you rather have something else? How about Chinese?" she suggested hopefully.

Three voices chorused emphatically, "Ugh! You promised pizza."

"Pizza twice in one week, princess? When you fall off the wagon, you really do take a tumble, don't you?" Mark taunted. "Am I going to have to roll you down the aisle?"

"What aisle?" Jeb demanded.

"Yeah, are you really marrying our Aunt Erin?"

"No," Erin declared just as Mark responded equally firmly, "You bet I am."

The boys looked confused.

"We have to work out the details," Mark explained with a grin. "In fact, you guys can be a big help."

"How?" Robby asked skeptically. As the oldest, he had developed a certain cynicism about seemingly innocent requests for help from adults. All too often, he'd discovered, they meant work.

"Well, your Aunt Erin isn't too sure about this yet. You can help me convince her. You can tell me all the things she likes most in the world, so I can try to win her over."

Erin glared at him with feigned severity. "Using innocent children to accomplish your own devious goals is not nice."

"I'm not using them," he protested. "I'm simply asking for their advice."

"Same difference."

"You're just worried that I'm going to win," he teased. "Well, all's fair in love and war, princess, and I intend to use any weapon I can find." He looked at the boys. "Can I count on your help, guys?"

Robby and Jeb looked at each other, while three-year-old Todd sat placidly sucking his thumb, a habit Maureen had been trying unsuccessfully to break. Apparently sensing there was some room for negotiation in Mark's request, Robby inquired, "Do we get pizza for dinner?"

"And hot-fudge sundaes for dessert?" Jeb suggested slyly.

Erin groaned as Mark nodded. "Sounds terrific to

me. Grab your coats, and let's get out of here. No fighting, either, or all bets are off."

The boys raced to the hall closet and grabbed their
jackets, the older ones for once actually helping Todd
with his instead of teasing him until he cried. Erin was
amazed.

"What about you, princess? Are you game?"

"Pizza? Hot-fudge sundaes? Do you have any idea
what it's going to be like trying to get through the night
after they've eaten all that? They'll have nightmares."

"You'll be here to comfort them."

"That's not the point."

"It sounds pretty good to me. I'd like to have you in
my bed comforting me," he said softly, his eyes warm-
ing as his gaze moved slowly over her body, leaving a
trail of fire in its wake.

"Mark!" she protested, but her response was weak-
ened by the heat that spread through her abdomen at the
sensual image he'd aroused.

"Come here," he suggested huskily.

She shook her head, but even as she did her feet
seemed to be propelled by some mysterious force. The
next moment she was in his arms, his lips velvet smooth
against hers, his arms steadying around her waist, his
hands massaging her back as her heart began its staccato
beat of desire.

"I love you," he whispered solemnly, his eyes shining.

"No," Erin protested, but the softly spoken denial
was captured by his mouth as his tongue slipped past
parted lips to the sweetness within. Hot. Hungry.
Demanding. He invaded her, stirred her to an aching
arousal, a desperate need. Her body pressed into his,
needing his warmth, his strength just to remain stand-

ing. She surrendered to the feelings he had brought to life in her, surrendered to the magical moment for once without thinking about the past or the future.

Abruptly, the sweet haze surrounding them was shattered by soft giggles and whispering.

"What're they doing?"

"Shh, dummy! Can't you see they're kissing?"

"Like Mommy and Daddy?"

"Yeah."

"But Mommy and Daddy are married."

Erin felt Mark's body start to quiver just before the roar of laughter erupted. "Puritanical little guys, aren't they?"

"They're merely concerned about my reputation," Erin replied loftily.

"Maybe," he said skeptically, still chuckling. "I suspect they're more concerned about when we're going to cut out the mushy stuff and get to the pizza." He glanced at the three grinning boys huddled in the doorway. "Right, guys?"

"Yeah! We're hungry!"

Mark cast a significant look in Erin's direction, a heated looked filled with sensuality and desire. "So am I, guys! So am I."

"You can have two desserts," Erin suggested sweetly.

"I intend to," he retorted, adding in a husky, taunting tone, "One while we're out and one when we get back."

"You wish," she replied, but her pulse rate shifted from low gear back to high at his seductive expression. It was enough to melt a hot-fudge sundae.

Or her heart.

- 8 -

MUCH LATER, WHEN Erin came downstairs from putting the boys to bed, Mark had a cozy fire blazing in the fireplace and was stretched out on the carpet in front of it. She stood silently for a moment and watched him, trying to understand all the conflicting feelings inside her.

On the one hand, she was delighted that he was so relaxed, so at ease with himself and with her, so comfortable in her environment. He had teased her affectionately all evening. He had laughed and joked easily with the boys, read them bedtime stories, and tucked them in as gently as if they were his own. It had been wonderful to see the instantaneous love and trust that had sprung up between him and her nephews.

On the other hand, she saw him now from a new, fascinating perspective: as a potential father, as well as a gentle and sensitive lover. In some ways, this new side of Mark was frightening simply because it threatened to shatter the last of her defenses.

She sighed softly at the beguiling sight of his hair glittering gold in the firelight and his slate-gray eyes gleaming like silver. Two precious metals. One intriguing, special man.

Mark had found Josh's brandy and poured them each a glass. When he spotted her in the doorway, he smiled invitingly and patted the carpet beside him. Despite the warning signals that shouted she should find a remote corner of the room to sit in, Erin settled down beside him and took the glass of amber liquid, thankful that, for the moment at least, he was not particularly talkative. She needed a few peaceful moments to regain her balance, to help her put into words the confusing thoughts that had been tumbling through her mind.

The first sip of brandy warmed her. The second eased her nervousness. The third loosened her tongue.

"You were very good with the boys tonight," she began.

"You sound surprised."

"I guess I am. I had the impression you don't have much of a family life."

Mark's eyes clouded over. "I did for a while," he said softly.

"What happened?"

"Erin, it was all a long time ago. Why talk about it now?"

"Because it's important."

"To you?"

"Yes," she said, adding more gently, "and to you. Did you have brothers and sisters?"

"No. There were just my parents and me."

She smiled at him and touched his cheek. "The only

son, huh? No wonder your father was so adamant about your taking over the family business. Why did you refuse?"

Mark sighed and turned away from her to stare thoughtfully into the fire. "A lot of reasons. I didn't want to be like my father, so caught up in business that I never knew what was happening around me. And, as I told you before, I wanted to be a cop."

"Why?"

"It was just something I needed to do because of something that happened."

To Erin's amazement, she saw tears shimmering in Mark's eyes. "What?" she pressed. "What happened?"

He was silent for so long, she thought he wasn't going to answer her. Finally, he began, "It was my mother. She . . . " He drew in a ragged breath. "She was killed by an intruder one night while my father was at one of his endless business meetings."

The breath rushed out of Erin in a harsh gasp of dismay. "Oh, Mark." She touched his shoulder and felt it tremble. "I'm so sorry. I had no idea. It must have been terrible."

"It was the worst time of my life," he said simply. "For a while I hated the world that could allow something like that to happen. And I hated my father because he wouldn't talk about it. He just withdrew into himself."

"And left you to handle it all alone."

He nodded. "I felt so helpless. I wanted to find the person who had done it, and I didn't know how."

"That's when you decided to become a policeman."

"Yes. My father was outraged. He thought it was beneath someone in our family. He got so furious, I finally told him I was willing to compromise. I said I would become a private investigator specializing in corporate theft. I thought that at least would be something he could understand. It would make use of that MBA he'd insisted I get and give me the satisfaction of helping people who'd been abused by crooks of one sort or another."

"Can I ask you a question?"

He grinned at her. "I haven't been able to stop you yet."

"I only know a little bit about what you do, but I have the feeling it's a very lonely life. Right?"

"In a way. You're always moving from one company to another. You can't make too many friends, because you're always looking for the bad guys and you can't afford to lose your objectivity."

"Are you sure that isn't the real reason you chose that career?"

Mark's brows knitted in a frown. "What do you mean?"

"I mean that it offers a perfect excuse for you to avoid being close to anyone so you won't get hurt again."

He gave her a shaky grin that wasn't at all convincing. "Practicing psychiatry without a license, aren't you?"

"Just giving you something to think about. I gather the compromise didn't satisfy your father."

"Nope. He said I was wasting my talents and until I came to my senses he didn't want to set eyes on me. I haven't seen him since."

Mark's cold words sent a shiver racing along Erin's spine. How could families turn away from each other like that? She thought of Mark all alone and trying to deal with his mother's murder, and it made her want to cry. Somehow he and his father had to be reconciled or he would never know any peace.

"Mark, don't you think it's time to try again? Families may get angry, but they never stop loving."

"In your family, maybe," he said bitterly. "Not in mine. Leave it alone, princess. It's been a long time, and I've learned to live with it."

"Have you really?" she said doubtfully.

"Yes," he said firmly, giving her a gentle smile. "And now I have you. I've stopped trying to find the answers to the past. You're the future, and you're all the family I need."

She looked at him curiously. "What about kids? Don't you want to have children of your own?"

"Of course, but I thought we ought to get the wedding out of the way first," he teased.

"Very funny. Are you so sure you're ready to give up your self-imposed isolation?"

"Oh, I'm ready. We're going to have a wonderful life with a whole slew of kids, just like Josh and Maureen."

"You mean tonight hasn't scared you off? You really had a good time?"

He chuckled at her obvious disbelief. "Of course. There's nothing like being around children to put things into their proper perspective. They see the world in such a fresh, untainted way. It's too bad we lose that as we grow older," he said wistfully.

"You didn't mind going to the noisiest pizza parlor in town and playing at least fifty video games before dinner?"

"Only when I lost."

"What about when Todd spilled his butterscotch sundae in your lap?"

He rolled his eyes. "I could have lived without that," he admitted.

Erin's eyes twinkled. "The waitress seemed only too willing to help you clean up the mess."

"Yes, she did, didn't she?" He glowered at her and added pointedly, "However, Ms. Matthews, if you had done something, instead of laughing like you'd just heard the ten best jokes of the century, I might not have needed her help."

"It was funny," she said, giggling again at the memory of his stunned expression as the twin rivers of vanilla ice cream and sticky golden butterscotch had run slowly down his pants. "Besides, you deserved it."

"How do you figure that?"

"You spent the entire evening pumping my nephews for information about me, and they—the little traitors —coughed it up without a qualm."

He grinned and scooted over so that he was close beside her. The next thing she knew she was leaning back comfortably against his chest, where she could smell the intoxicatingly masculine scent of him and feel the strong, reassuring beat of his heart. His warmth radiated through her, and the casual touch of his hand, which rested just below her breast, sent shivers tripping along her spine. Her breath, which had been so even only a moment before, caught in her throat at his nearness, his devastating assault on her senses. Another few minutes or a slight slip of his hand and he'd have her panting for more. Mark, blast him, seemed perfectly oblivious to her reaction.

"They did, didn't they?" he was saying, chuckling delightedly at the long list of revelations that had come amid the boys' giggles and Erin's blushes. "I had absolutely no idea you could play 'Yankee Doodle' on the comb."

"It's not something I share with the world," she retorted haughtily.

"I'd like to hear it."

"Forget it."

"How about tossing a Frisbee? Will you do that with me in the park one day?"

"We'll see."

"Or maybe you'd rather show me your collection of baseball cards?" he said with a leer.

The man was getting entirely too smug. One evening of titillating revelations about Aunt Erin's secrets, including her passion for Monopoly and root beer floats, and he thought he knew everything there was to know about her.

But he didn't know her at all. Not really. He still didn't understand why she couldn't trust him, couldn't trust these feelings that were growing between them. Terry had known all those crazy habits and obsessions, too—had even shared many of her secret passions— and look what had happened with that. Merely confessing to a love of baseball cards, Monopoly, and root beer floats was no basis for a relationship, much less a marriage.

"Penny for your thoughts, princess."

"Haven't you heard about inflation?"

"Don't avoid the subject. Why were you looking so pensive?"

"Mark, we're getting closer and closer—"

"I'm glad you're ready to admit that much at least."

"Stop it. You know what I mean. Physically, there's obviously an attraction between us, but that's not enough."

"I never suggested it was."

"We need time."

"We have four days left," he said with an aplomb that irritated the daylights out of her.

"That is not time!" she snapped. "That's an impossible, unreasonable deadline."

Mark's hand was trailing along her cheek as she talked, making further thought difficult. When his fingers traced a delicate path down her neck and over her shoulder, Erin found that she was holding her breath, waiting for his touch to reach the suddenly aching need of her breasts.

"Mark," she protested, "this is no answer."

"It's a start," he murmured softly, his lips following the same trail blazed by his fingers. When his mouth captured her taut, swollen nipple, a shudder ripped through her. Through the cotton of her blouse she could feel the moistness of his demanding suckling, and she arched toward it. His fingers fumbled with the buttons of her shirt, slowly exposing her braless breasts to his greedy view. His soft sigh was a whisper of utter delight.

"You're so lovely. Cool, pale satin with fire beneath."

His eyes met hers, refused to let her look away in embarrassment or confusion. His gaze demanded that she yield to him, that she admit the same longings he was expressing with his words, his touch, the tension in his body.

"Please," he urged softly.

Erin's voice was shaky, her body suddenly beyond her control, responding with a will of its own to the needs he aroused in her. "Please what?"

"Love me, princess. Let me love you."

Her thundering heart told her to say yes, the wildfire that was building in her abdomen demanded it, and yet . . .

And yet she was afraid. Terrified, in fact. Once she had known the joy of being in Mark's arms, of feeling that excitement of his touch, would she ever be able to view their situation rationally again? Absolutely not. It would be as impossible as trying to get the moon to rise in the morning or the rain to go back to the clouds. It would change things forever, and it wasn't a change she was brave enough to face. Not yet, anyway.

"I can't," she told him softly, reluctantly.

"Can't or won't?"

"Does it make a difference?"

"I think so."

"Then I'm not sure which it is. I only know that this is still wrong for me."

"Because you're afraid?"

She nodded. There was no point in denying the truth.

"Princess, you don't ever have to be afraid of me."

"But I'm not," she responded, surprised that he thought that. "I'm afraid of me, of letting myself feel again." It was an admission that cost her, but Mark apparently understood.

"You're afraid of being hurt again."

"Yes."

He took a deep, shaky breath and sat away from her, as though afraid of where further contact might lead him. "Do you want to tell me about your marriage?"

"There's nothing to tell, really. It was just a case of two people who were all wrong for each other finding that out too late."

"So that you've never been able to trust your instincts again?"

"Exactly."

"What do your instincts tell you about me?"

Erin looked into Mark's eyes and found the courage to be honest. "That you're warm and sensitive and intelligent. That you're fun to be with and dependable. That you're strong and courageous."

"Do your instincts also tell you that I love you very much?"

"Yes."

He smiled at her slowly, complacently. "Then I'd say you have very good instincts."

She chuckled. "You would."

He ran a finger across her bare breast, teasing the nipple to a hardened peak. "I don't suppose I'm going to convince you to trust them tonight, am I?"

"I want to, Mark," she told him solemnly. "I do want to."

"That's a good beginning," he said, carefully buttoning her blouse with trembling fingers. The brush of his warm touch against her sensitive skin almost made her change her mind, but she bit her lip and remained silent. When her blouse was buttoned, he handed her a snifter of brandy and took a sip of his own.

"Mark."

"Yes?"

"It really is a start," she promised, admitting to him —and to herself—what she wanted for the future. Their future.

Before he could answer, the phone rang, shattering their moment of intimacy. Erin went to answer it, returning a few minutes later, her expression troubled.

"It's for you. It's Jean-Pierre."

While Mark was out of the room, she sat on the edge of the sofa, her hands balled into fists so tight that her knuckles had turned white. The call was trouble. She just knew it. Jean-Pierre had tried to sound cheerful, but she had detected the nervousness in his voice. Something had happened or was going to happen. Worse, Mark was going to be right in the thick of it.

When he came back into the room, she didn't even have to hear the words or see his jacket to know he was leaving.

"What's happened?"

"The thieves came back again."

"Is Jean-Pierre okay?"

"He's fine, but they got away with one of his works tonight. I almost think he'd rather be beaten up than lose one of those crazy pieces of sculpture."

Oddly, Erin could understand that. She might think they were perfectly awful, but those creations were a part of him, perhaps not in quite the same way as a child, but a part of him nonetheless. It would be shattering to see something like that stolen or destroyed.

"Tell him I'm sorry," she said sincerely.

"We're going to get it back."

She studied him. "The way you say that, it almost sounds as though you know where it is."

"We have an idea."

"Mark, you don't seriously mean you're going after it?"

"Yes. That's exactly what we're doing."

"But . . ."

"Shh," he said, pulling her into his arms. "It's going to be just fine."

"Mark, if anything happens to you, I'll . . . I'll . . ."

"Drown yourself in root beer floats?" he teased, obviously trying to lighten the moment, to relieve her tension. His attempt failed.

"It's not funny." she snapped.

"I'm glad you feel that way," he said, kissing her hungrily until Erin felt her nervousness slip away, to be replaced by another type of tension entirely. His lips created a warmth inside her that built quickly, finally exploding into white-hot flames that devoured her. She wanted to hold him, to cling to him and prevent him from leaving, from walking into danger.

But she let him go.

"Night, princess," he said before closing the front door.

She pressed her face against the windowpane and watched him hurry into the darkness. "Be careful, my love," she whispered into the suddenly lonely silence.

- 9 -

"WHERE'S UNCLE MARK?" Jeb inquired at breakfast the following morning.

"He's not your uncle Mark," Erin replied peevishly. Her head had been throbbing, ever since Mark had left to go chasing around in the dead of night after a bunch of thieves. The kids' noise and their endless questions weren't doing a thing to relieve the pounding. "And I don't know where he is."

"Didn't he stay here last night?" Jeb's face fell in disappointment.

"No, dummy," Robby chimed in. "He can't stay here if he and Aunt Erin aren't married."

"Why not?"

"Never mind," Erin said, putting plates of scrambled eggs in front of Jeb and Robby.

"Want my orange juice," Todd demanded, responding to the tense mood by banging a spoon on the table.

"Todd, stop that this instant!" Erin yelled, slamming the juice down and watching it splatter across the table.

"My, my. It must have been quite an evening." Maureen's cheerful observation created an uproar as three children temporarily deserted the breakfast Erin had prepared to embrace their mother and excitedly tell her all about Uncle Mark and their dinner of pizza and hot-fudge sundaes. Maureen's eyebrows rose.

"Don't look at me," Erin said. "*Uncle* Mark chose the menu."

"Couldn't you have stopped him? They'll be hyperactive for a week."

"How can you tell? They're always hyperactive."

Maureen looked at her curiously. "What's bugging you?"

"Uncle Mark didn't spend the night," Jeb offered ingenuously through a mouthful of scrambled eggs.

Maureen grinned. "Oh," she said significantly. "I see."

"You do not see," Erin retorted.

Something in Erin's voice apparently got through to Maureen, because she immediately said, "Boys, finish getting ready for school."

"Mom . . ."

"You heard me. March."

When they had reluctantly left the room, she poured herself a cup of coffee and sat down opposite Erin. "Okay, Sis. What's up?"

Erin lifted worried brown eyes to meet her sister's concerned gaze. "Mark went barreling out of here last night to track down some thieves who'd made off with a piece of Jean-Pierre's sculpture, and I haven't heard a word from him since. I'm worried sick about him."

"Mark strikes me as the type of man who can take

care of himself. Stop worrying," Maureen said so calmly that Erin wanted to shake her. Being the mother of three wildly adventurous boys must do something to your mind, she decided.

"Does he also strike you as the type of man who'd have sense enough to call someone he claims to love to let her know he's okay?"

"Maybe he hasn't had time. Or maybe he doesn't think the woman in question cares what happens to him," Maureen said slyly.

Erin glared at her and snapped, "Or maybe he's hurt. Or just plain inconsiderate." She moaned. "Damn. I knew I shouldn't start to trust him. I just knew it."

Maureen banged her coffee cup down. "Good Lord, Erin, give the man a chance. He left here when?"

"I don't know. It was sometime after midnight, I guess."

"And it is now barely seven in the morning. Isn't it possible that he thought any of those hours in between might be just the slightest bit too late or too early to call?" she suggested reasonably.

"I suppose," Erin said doubtfully. "Do you really think he's okay?"

"I'm sure of it," Maureen said confidently. "Why don't you call him? Or is that concept too liberated for you?"

"Frankly, I hadn't even thought of it."

"You're too used to suffering in silence, little sister. Stand up and fight."

Erin grinned at her. "Have you and Josh ever thought of writing a book on relationships? Between you, you've cornered the market on practical wisdom for the eighties."

"Suggesting a phone call to put your mind at rest is

hardly unique practical wisdom."

"But you always seem to know how to drag me back to reality and get me to focus on the issues."

"That's because we know you and we're able to be a little more objective about your situation than you are. You're so busy trying not to fall in love, you can't see that it's too late. You're a goner, little sister."

"I am not in love with Mark," Erin denied heatedly, not yet prepared to define her feelings that clearly.

"Oh, yes, you are," Maureen said smugly.

"Am not."

"Are, too."

"Am not," Erin repeated, finally giggling at their quick reversion to childhood taunting. "Okay," she admitted. "Maybe I do care about him just a little."

"Humph!"

"Okay. A lot."

"Why don't you give the man a break and tell him that?"

Erin sighed. "Maybe I will . . . if I ever see him again."

"Erin!"

"Yes, ma'am. When I see him again."

Maureen's expression was that of a thoroughly satisfied cat who'd just discovered a whole bowl of rich cream. "That's better." She paused, then suggested far too casually, "Why don't you try calling him now?"

Erin groaned. "Give me a break."

"Nope. Somebody's got to push you or you'll spend the rest of your life shut up in that studio apartment with a bed that squeaks. You really need to do something about that, by the way. Someone downstairs kept pounding on the ceiling all night long."

Erin chuckled. "All night?"

Maureen blushed furiously. "You know what I mean."

"Oh, I think I know exactly what you mean."

"Get off my case, little sister. We're trying to straighten out your life, not mine."

"It doesn't sound like yours needs any help."

"It doesn't, thank the Lord, and stop trying to change the subject. Call Mark."

"Okay. Okay." Just as Erin reached for the wall phone, it rang. She grabbed it before the second ring. "Hello. Yes."

"Hi, princess."

Erin breathed a sigh of relief. "You're okay?"

"Just fine except for some bumps and bruises."

Her heart skidded to a stop. "Bumps and bruises?"

"I tripped over a ladder."

"Trying to climb onto some Juliet's balcony?"

"No, wise guy. Trying to sneak through an alley."

"Did you find the sculpture?"

"More or less."

"What does that mean?"

"By the time we got to it, it looked a little more like scrap metal than Jean-Pierre's usual work."

"Oh, my. Jean-Pierre must be beside himself."

"I'd say furious is a more accurate description. I would not like to be in the thief's shoes if our artist friend ever bumps into him. He's liable to murder him with his palette knife, and in case you've never seen one, those things have a very dull edge."

Erin shuddered, even though she knew Mark was kidding. She had a feeling the whole incident had been much more dangerous than Mark was letting on.

"Erin, I've got to run. I just wanted to let you know I was okay and that I'll see you tonight."

"There you go again," she retorted with feigned anger.

"There I go again what?"

"Making plans without asking me."

"You asked me."

"I did?"

"Sure," he said innocently. "You promised to let me help you rehearse your love scene. I can hardly wait."

"Mark . . ." she began, but he was already gone. And, despite herself, a thrill of anticipation had shot through her. They had had that particular discussion before last night, and last night she had discovered just how susceptible she was to Mark's caresses. And if she had to lay odds on it, she'd bet that last night had been only a dress rehearsal for tonight. It was going to take every ounce of willpower she possessed to say no to Mark a second time.

Erin spent the rest of the day practicing, but it wasn't her lines she was rehearsing. She was trying to find the words that would keep her safely out of Mark's arms. By the time he finally rang her doorbell, she'd realized that the reason such scripting had seemed so elusive was that deep inside she didn't want to say no again. She wanted one perfect night with him before they had to say an inevitable good-bye.

When she opened the door to find him standing there in snug jeans and one of those sweat shirts that emphasized every muscle in his arms and shoulders, the last of her good resolutions went up in smoke. The man was gorgeous, far too virile for a mere mortal woman to resist.

"Hi," he said, planting a solid kiss on her mouth before heading straight to the kitchen and grabbing a handful of the crackers she'd put on a plate.

"Aren't you going to wait for the cheese?" she inquired tartly.

"I figured you'd fed it to the mouse."

"I saved some for the rat."

He shook his head. "Not nice, princess," he chided her as he settled down on the sofa and gazed up at her with a wicked twinkle in his eye. There was an implicit dare in that look, and it made Erin's blood roar.

"Okay," he said cheerfully. "What do we do?"

Erin regarded him nervously. "Are you sure you want to do this?"

"You bet. I can hardly wait."

"That's what I was afraid of," she muttered, handing him a script. "You read Darryl's part, and I'll do my part."

"I hope so, princess," he said fervently.

"Mark!"

"Sorry. Where do you want me to start?"

"Start with 'Jennifer, I can't stay away from you anymore.'"

He leered at her, and a tingle shot along her spine. This wasn't going to work. They hadn't even read the first lines yet, and already her body was reacting as though it were on hormone supplements. Why did he have to look so blasted attractive, so much sexier than the actor with whom she'd have to play the scene on Monday?

His hair had been ruffled by the wind, and his cheeks were filled with the color of outdoors. Those damn designer jeans clung to his narrow hips and to lanky, muscular legs that she remembered from her aerobics class as being covered with a golden haze of hair. That casual, sleeveless sweat shirt that displayed every curve of his strong, powerful arms was in a shade of dark gray that matched his eyes. He'd kicked off his Gucci loafers and made himself perfectly at home. Except it was her home, and Mark tended to dominate it. She had the strangest desire to stick her head out the window and take a gulp of the crisp, reviving fall air outside, but her windows had been stuck for years, thanks to repeated, careless painting by former tenants. She took a sip of root beer instead. It didn't help.

"'Jennifer, I can't stay away from you anymore.'"

"What?" Erin said blankly. "Who's Jennifer?"

"You are. Aren't you paying attention?"

"Sorry. I guess not. Let's try it again."

"'Jennifer, I can't stay away from you anymore.'"

"'Darryl, you must. Too many people will be hurt if we give in to our passions.'"

"Who writes this stuff?"

"Mark!"

"Okay. Okay," he said, glancing down at his script. "'But, darling, we were meant for each other.'"

"'No. We have our own lives now. There is no place in mine for you.'"

"'Are you so sure of that?'" Mark looked at Erin curiously. "Don't you think I should kiss you here?"

"What?" she replied, wetting her lips nervously.

"It seems like the perfect opening for a kiss," he said hopefully.

"Does the script say anything about a kiss?"

"No."

"Then forget it."

"I still think we ought to try it. If it works, you can suggest it to the director." He slid toward her on the sofa and repeated the line slowly. "'Are you so sure of that?'"

He leaned toward her and touched her still-damp lips

gently with his own. When she gasped at the fleeting, thoroughly sensual contact, he deepened the kiss until Erin could feel her body strain toward him. Her script fell from her hands as she reached out to wrap her arms around him.

Suddenly, before she could curl her fingers in the fine golden silk of his hair, he sat back. "Yes. I definitely think that's better. Go ahead now."

"Go ahead?" Erin's brain seemed to have turned into cornmeal mush. Not a single rational thought could work its way through her mind to her lips.

"With your line."

"Oh." She picked the script up off the floor and fumbled with it until she found the scene again. "'I'm sure,'" she said with much less conviction than she was certain the writer had intended.

"'Perhaps I can convince you to change your mind.'"

"'No,'" she insisted. "'I will never change my mind. Not with so much at stake. Please, Darryl, you must leave now.'"

"'Not without one last kiss.'"

Gray eyes gazed into hers. "'One last kiss,'" he repeated softly, his breath a tantalizing whisper across her lips. Darryl. No, it was Mark, definitely Mark, who seemed to be holding himself back, refusing to close that infinitesimal gap that separated them, waiting for her to make the choice.

Jennifer might have had a choice, but Erin had none. Once again her script slipped to the floor as her hands reached out to clasp Mark's head and draw his mouth down on hers. She kissed him with a desperate urgency, a hunger that stunned her at first. Stunned both of them. She heard Mark's gasp of surprise, then his ragged breathing as he claimed her with his feverish lips, his rasping tongue.

For just a moment he pulled back and looked at her, asking a silent question, reading her response in her eyes. Then, slowly, he slipped her sweater over her head and blazed a path across her shoulders, down the gentle cleft between her breasts. The dusky rose of Erin's nipples darkened as his thumb rubbed them into sensitive buds, which flowered into ripples of demanding heat.

Stretched out on the sofa, Erin was ready for him, waiting and hungry as his hands and mouth worshipped every inch of her bared skin. When he had paid homage to each breast, he unsnapped her jeans, then slid the zipper down, allowing his hand to linger on the white-hot mound of her femininity.

"Mark, please. Hurry," she urged, her hips arching into the palm of his hand.

"Not so fast, princess. I want to get to know every inch of you."

Slowly and tenderly he explored her receptive body, finding each and every spot that pushed her toward a peak of excitement. For Erin it was a glorious, once-in-a-lifetime experience, this rapid, exhilarating climb followed by a gradual descent, then another race to the top.

Just when she expected him to take her over the edge, he pulled away.

"Mark?"

"Hush, princess. Let's open this bed of yours and do this right."

Erin stood on shaky legs while Mark hurriedly tossed the pillows out of the way and opened the studio couch. At last he allowed her to slip his clothes off so that she could feast her eyes on the firmness of his body, his powerful masculinity. Together they sank down onto the bed, her hands eagerly touching the warm, supple skin that burned like fire, her mouth seeking the salty taste of his tangy flesh. A moan tore through him as her fingers swooped low to capture him, to taunt him.

"Now, Mark," she pleaded again.

"Now," he agreed, lowering himself to her with deliberately provocative hesitation. "Now," he said softly again as he thrust himself inside at last, their joining creating a powerful surge that took them both to the top and back again.

The primitive motion felt as natural as breathing and far more exciting. Mark's murmured words of endearment, his exquisitely sensual pace—first rapid and then tantalizingly slow—his constantly exploring fingers all combined to wind the coil of tension inside her ever tighter. Her body arched to meet each thrust. Her hands raked down his spine, dug into his shoulders. And when an explosion of sheer delight ripped through her, her teeth bit into his shoulder as she muffled her shout of joy and awe.

Dear God, Erin thought as she lay drenched in perspiration in Mark's arms. She felt exhilarated yet . . . what? Safe, as though she'd come home at last. How will I ever let him go now? she wondered desperately. It was just as she had feared: She had discovered that their opposite natures made a perfect, satisfying whole. Yet she still had so many doubts.

Mark kissed her softly, persistently, and the doubts vanished again. "Now you've done it, princess."

"Done what?"

"The spell is complete. If you leave me now, I'll turn into a frog."

Studying him with mock solemnity, Erin retorted,

"That really would be too bad. Green is definitely not your color."

"Cute."

She leaned down to gently touch her lips to the spot she had nipped earlier. "Maybe there's still time to do something about it."

"Like what?"

Her kisses fanned across his chest, then followed the golden path of his hair down. "Like this."

Mark moaned. "I like your ideas, princess."

"Are you sure?" she taunted, holding herself just a fraction of an inch away.

"I'm sure."

"Show me."

And for the rest of the night, he did.

- *10* -

ERIN WAS AWAKENED early Saturday morning by the ringing of the doorbell. Her body returned from its languorous state slowly and reluctantly. When she tried to crawl out of bed to answer the blasted ringing, she found she couldn't move. One very strong arm was curved protectively across her midsection.

"Mark!" She tried to shake him.

"Yes," he mumbled and rolled toward her, capturing her even more tightly against his body. Sparks flew between them. Again. "Love you."

Erin wanted to lie right there and savor those words, but the ringing now alternated with a pounding that was going to have Mrs. Bates and the rest of the neighbors down on her head. She nudged Mark again.

"Mark," she said loudly in his ear, "someone is at the door."

"Go 'way."

Terrific. She'd fallen for a man who was incoherent until noon. "They are not going away. They are getting angry," she said emphatically, trying to slide out of his embrace. He held on tighter. She wriggled harder, an action that stirred a responsive moan from Mark and sent a jolt of electricity coursing through her. It was a reaction she had to ignore. She wriggled some more. When she'd finally negotiated her escape, she looked down at him and sighed. He was sprawled facedown, right across the middle of the bed, his breathing once more steady and even. Asleep. The man was sound asleep again.

Thoroughly irritated, she yanked her pink nightgown and robe out of the closet and pulled them on.

"Who is it?" she called out finally, trying to make herself heard over the combined pounding and ringing.

"Mid-morning Madness."

"Who?"

"Mid-morning Madness."

Was this some sort of bizarre practical joke? It was hardly mid-morning, and the only madness with which she had any familiarity was the wildly passionate love-making that had filled the night. "I don't know anyone by that name."

"Lady, it's not my name," the man snapped back, not bothering to mask his disgust for the sake of good customer relations. "It's the company. Now, open the door and let me give you this bloody breakfast, so I can get on to my next delivery."

Erin peeked through the peephole and saw a thoroughly disgruntled man dressed in a tuxedo, carrying a wicker tray covered with a variety of dishes and one gorgeous, perfect, long-stemmed red rose. The scowling man and his presumably pleasurable mission seemed to be at odds. She wondered if he often encountered such grouchy, disbelieving customers.

Still, she had to ask, "Are you sure you have the right address?"

"Are you Erin Matthews?"

"Yes."

"Then I have the right address. Now, are you going to open the door, or shall I dump this tray out here on the floor?"

Erin opened the door.

"Where do you want it?"

She considered having him dump it on Mark's head, but the aroma of fresh coffee got to her. "Over there," she suggested, gesturing toward the kitchen counter. She dug in her purse and came up with a tip. "Thanks."

"Any time, lady. This is what I'm in business for."

"What do I do with the tray?"

"It's all yours. Your husband paid enough for it."

"Husband?" She glanced at Mark. "Oh." She started to correct him, then thought better of it. It was none of this man's business who that semicomatose nut in her bed was.

When the waiter had gone, she peeked into all the containers on the tray. Eggs Benedict. Croissants. Strawberry jam. Grapefruit juice. Coffee. A feast fit for a king. Or a prince and his princess. Suddenly she was ravenous.

"What's that?" Mark mumbled sleepily, his eyes still closed so that Erin wasn't sure if he was truly awake or merely muttering in his sleep.

"Breakfast."

"Where'd it come from?"

"That's what I'd like to know," she replied tartly.

"The man said something about my husband ordering it."

Mark's eyes flew open.

"I thought that might wake you up."

"I'd forgotten."

"I'll bet," she responded skeptically. "Awfully sure of yourself, weren't you?"

"Not at all." Innocent gray eyes met her doubtful gaze evenly. "I was planning to arrive with the waiter."

"Of course you were."

"Princess, your doubts are cruel. I had no way of knowing you were finally going to succumb to my charms last night," he said, propping himself up against the pillows, the sheet flung haphazardly across him so that he seemed decidedly provocative rather than just decently covered. Erin's heart lurched, and breakfast seemed less and less enticing. "Well?"

"Well what?" she said blankly, her eyes riveted to the bare expanse of his chest.

"Are you going to bring that breakfast back to bed so we can share it?"

"You could come and get it."

He grinned at her, and one bare leg poked its way out from under the sheet.

"Never mind," she said hurriedly. "I'll bring it."

The food was surprisingly good, but what stunned Erin even more was her total lack of self-consciousness as she and Mark sat in bed and lingered over the coffee and croissants. She told herself that the intimacy should have disturbed her, but instead it felt right. Very right. As though they'd been doing this for a lifetime.

"What do you want to do today?" he asked finally.

"I need to leave for the museum in a half hour," she

told him, glancing at the clock. "Josh will be waiting for me downstairs."

"No, he won't."

"He won't?"

"I told him you'd be taking the day off and spending it with me," he said calmly, reaching over for the last of her croissant.

Erin's temper went straight into orbit. "You had no right!"

He looked her squarely in the eye, ignoring her furious tone. "I had every right, princess. I only have a few days left to convince you to marry me, and I'm not going to allow you out of my sight until you've said yes."

"But I have a responsibility to pay Josh back."

"And you will. One Saturday is not going to make that big a difference."

"That's not your decision to make. You should have discussed it with me."

"Would you have said yes?"

"No."

He shrugged pointedly. "That's why I had to take drastic measures."

Erin knew that one day really wouldn't make that much difference. But Mark's arrogance in assuming he could just take over her life grated on her nerves. He had to learn that she was her own woman, that no man told her what to do, even one with whom she was falling in love.

"I'm going to the museum," she said adamantly.

Mark's eyes blazed back at her with passion. "Are you really?" he taunted, reaching over to caress her silk-covered breast. A ripple of heat washed over her, weakening her vehemence.

"Yes."

"Are you sure?" he said, his gaze locked with hers as his fingers continued to dance across her flesh.

"Okay. Okay," she relented with a breathless laugh. "You win. This time."

He grinned, obviously pleased with the victory. "So what would you like to do?"

"Surprise me."

"I thought I always surprised you," he murmured huskily, moving the breakfast tray to the side of the bed and pulling her back into the haven of his arms. His fingers skimmed across the silk of her gown, tantalizing the flesh beneath. He slipped the robe from her shoulders, then sprinkled kisses across her skin. The tiny straps of her nightgown were next, and the pink silk fell away to expose the paler satin of her skin. As his lips captured her already taut nipple, Erin uttered a low moan and swept away the sheet that had shielded Mark from her eager view and touch.

This time when they made love, she was more abandoned than she'd ever been in her life, taking, demanding, urging satisfaction . . . for herself and for him. Each touch became a fiery weapon of arousal, as taunting as the flame that lures a moth. She couldn't get enough of him, of his hair-roughened skin teasing her flesh, of his murmured words of passion and excitement . . . of love, of the joyous unity of their perfectly attuned bodies.

When she had settled into the curve of his body again, replete with the wondrousness of their joining, she sighed softly. "We could do this all day," she suggested.

"Don't you think you'd get bored after a while?"

"Never," she said fervently, still awed at the way Mark had made her feel, at the emotions that were surging to life in her after only one week with this incredibly loving man.

"Does that mean you'll consider keeping me around?"

She hesitated thoughtfully. "Well . . ."

"Erin!"

She nipped him playfully on the shoulder and felt yet another shudder rip through him. "I'll consider it," she promised.

"In the meantime, I have a few ideas for the rest of the day."

"What are they?"

"Uh-uh. You said you wanted to be surprised."

"Mark, you said we were going sailing."

"We are."

"But this is Central Park."

"Very observant."

"You can't sail in Central Park."

"Sure you can . . . if you believe in magic."

"Magic?"

"You see this bag I have here?"

"Yes."

"Well, inside this magical bag, I have a sailing vessel that can carry us across the sea."

"Right."

"Close your eyes."

"Mark."

"Close 'em."

"Okay. But I still think you're crazy."

"Of course I am. Now open your eyes."

"That's a toy sailboat!"

"Not if you believe hard enough."

* * *

"I told you that boat wasn't magic."

"Your skepticism wounds me, princess."

"It sank like a rock."

"So, its magical powers had an off day. Nobody's perfect."

"What else do you have in that bag of tricks?"

"A dragon."

"You're going to slay a dragon for me? That really is impressive."

"Cute."

"You're not going to slay a dragon?"

"You're going to fly one."

"I beg your pardon."

"It's a kite, princess. You're going to fly it."

"There's no wind."

"Of course there is. There's always a breeze in October."

"Mark, there is no breeze."

"Then you'll just have to run faster, won't you, princess?"

"You broke my dragon."

"It's your fault. I told you I couldn't run fast enough to make that silly thing stay up in the sky."

"Actually, you looked pretty cute sprawled out on the ground with that pink and orange tail tangled around your sexy legs."

"That's because you have a perverted sense of humor. By the way, are you planning on feeding me? I'm starving."

"For a woman who lived on rabbit food until a few days ago, you've certainly developed an appetite."

"Mmm. I have, haven't I?"

"Princess! We're in public."

"Too bad, isn't it?"

"Definitely."

"Maybe we could go home for just a little while."

"You're insatiable."

"Are you complaining?"

"No way."

"Princess."

"Yes."

"Now I'm starved."

"For food?"

"Yes, you wanton little wench."

"How about if I take you out for a gourmet meal?"

"I'll have to go home and change."

"No, you won't. Not for the place I have in mind."

"Princess, what are we doing back in Central Park?"

"Just sit down."

"But you promised me a gourmet meal."

"Don't pout. You'll have one in just a minute. Close your eyes."

"Why did I like it better when you had your eyes closed?"

"Because you like being in control. Now it's my turn. I'll be back in a minute."

"Where are you going? Princess! Princess!!"

"Quiet, Mark, or you'll have the mounted police in here after us."

"Thank goodness you're back. Where have you been?"

"Getting dinner."

"You got a gourmet meal in ten minutes?"

"I was only gone five. It just seemed longer because you missed me."

"No. It seemed longer because I'm famished."

"Never fear. Your dinner awaits."

"Hot dogs?"

"With sauerkraut and mustard."

"Soft pretzels?"

"And ice cream. We'd better eat the ice cream first or it'll melt all over us."

"We could lick it off."

"Now, that's an idea."

"Mark, the hot dogs are cold."

"You're the one who wanted to turn eating ice cream into a sensuous experience."

"You suggested it."

"But I was kidding."

"You weren't kidding a minute ago."

"That's true, princess. That was very serious. Now, what about my other idea?"

"No, I will not go swimming with you."

"Come on, princess. It'll be fun."

"Mark, it is sixty degrees out here. It's too cold and too dark to go swimming. Besides, I'm not about to go out into that lake with who knows what floating around in it."

"I wasn't thinking of the lake."

"What then? Do you belong to a health club with a heated indoor pool?"

"Not exactly."

"Mark . . ."

"Come on, princess. You're going to love it."

"Mark, we're going to be arrested."

"Why? All we're doing is enjoying the fountain."

"I think you're supposed to stand on the sidewalk to

enjoy it, not dance around under the spray."

"Princess, don't go stuffy on me now. It's beautiful in here. It's like being surrounded by a curtain of twinkling lights."

"Do they remind you at all of the bars on a jail cell?"

"I don't know. I've never been in jail. I think they're more like Christmas tree lights."

"Mark, you're going to catch pneumonia."

"You're wavering, princess. I can tell. I wouldn't catch pneumonia if you were in here with me. In fact, if you were in here with me, we could turn this into a steam bath."

"Very funny. Is it really beautiful in there?"

"It really is."

"Mark, put me down. You're soaking wet. Mark! Oh, Mark! You're right. It's . . . it's magical."

"Told you."

"It's also freezing."

"Come here, princess. I'll keep you warm."

"Mark, did you see the expression on that policeman's face when we climbed out of that fountain dripping wet and sloshed off down the street?" Erin asked, giggling at the memory.

"I think it was the look of yet another man who'd been bewitched by my princess."

"More likely the look of a man torn between carrying out his civic responsibility and having hysterics," she retorted, suddenly shivering in the cool night air. Mark immediately drew her into his arms and pressed her into his body heat.

"You need to take a hot shower."

"Are you coming in with me?" she asked hopefully.

"I'm already waterlogged."

"I could make it worth your while."

Mark gave an exaggerated moan. "Lord, I've created a monster."

An hour later they were propped up in bed with steaming mugs of hot chocolate, their legs barely touching under the covers. The contact was just enough to spark Erin's awareness of the man beside her, of the man who had bewitched her in just one short week. She had done what she had sworn she would never do: She had fallen for Mark and his captivating sense of the absurd, his whimsical approach to life. Her own more rational approach to things had wavered somewhere between their sailing excursion and dinner in the park. It had vanished completely in the fountain, washed away by what Mark had sworn was a shower of starlight around them. It had been a perfect day, a day for falling in love.

"Mark, thank you."

"For what?"

"For giving me today."

"There are thousands more where that came from, princess," he whispered softly, taking the mug from her hands and pulling her unresisting body gently into his arms. "Tomorrow we'll have another one."

- *11* -

It was noon on another picture-perfect fall day by the time they ventured out of Erin's apartment on Sunday.

As they headed for a popular neighborhood restaurant for brunch, she grumbled, "I don't know why you insisted on going out when I could have fixed breakfast at home. You want to marry me, and you don't even know if I can cook."

"That wasn't a prerequisite. We can live on love," Mark said airily.

"I want you to remember that when I burn the biscuits to a crisp and ruin the roast."

Mark suddenly stopped in his tracks and gazed down at her, his eyes bright. "Does that mean what I think it means?"

"What?"

"That you're finally saying yes?"

"To what?"

"Marriage."

"No. Of course not."

"What do you mean, of course not? I thought after yesterday you were finally ready to admit that you love me."

Erin shifted uncomfortably from one foot to the other and tried to avoid Mark's penetrating gaze. "I do love you," she said finally. "At least, I think I do. It's hard to tell if anything is real when you're in the middle of being swept off your feet."

A grin lit up his face. "Swept off your feet, huh?"

"Don't get cocky, hero. It may be only a temporary aberration on my part."

"You know it's not, princess. You're down for the count, too."

"So what happens now?"

He took her hand and pulled her along. "First we have brunch, and then we do some more of your favorite things, just to make sure you won't change your mind."

"What about your favorite things?"

"If you're happy, then I've got everything I need."

In the crowded restaurant, they waited nearly twenty minutes, but at last they were able to get a booth so they could sit across from each other and rub knees under the table. Unfortunately the contact made Erin's hands shake so badly, she could scarcely lift her coffee to her mouth without spilling it. Every nerve in her body was alive and attuned to Mark's dazzling presence across from her.

The fact that he was not only able to down a he-man's portion of pancakes, eggs, bacon, and sausage, but calmly read the Sunday paper irritated the daylights out of her. Why couldn't he be half as nervous about what was happening between them as she was? Weren't men the ones who were supposed to run from commitments? Instead, he was treating the whole idea of marriage as though it were as simple, clear cut, and uneventful as choosing between orange and grapefruit juice. This morning Erin hadn't even been able to do that. Amused by her flustered indecisiveness, Mark had finally ordered apple juice for her.

How could everyone except her be so certain that this was right? Even her family had taken to Mark instantaneously, with none of the doubts that had colored their initial reaction to Terry. They had never thought Terry was right for her, though they had carefully refrained from a chorus of "I told you so's" when things had fallen apart. It was a total contrast to their welcoming of Mark into the fold. They were practically throwing her into his arms, and she knew it wasn't because they were simply desperate to see her married again. Josh and Maureen genuinely liked and trusted Mark. They had seen the substance, the genuine caring beneath the whimsy. For that matter, so had she. So why couldn't she take that final leap of faith to commitment?

It was the past again, of course. As much as she'd tried to put it behind her, it was still ever-present in her mind, a constant reminder that her judgment had been incredibly lousy once and could be again. As she had told Mark already, her instincts were telling her that he was sensitive, strong, and dependable, but she still doubted her instincts. In spite of her love, which had flowered into full blossom yesterday without a single cloud of doubt to shadow their perfect day, today she was nervous again and unsure. She was unwilling to take that irrevocable step toward total commitment.

It was as though marriage itself were the stumbling

block. If they could simply remain together always as they had been for the last week, life would be wonderful. But there was something about the idea of vowing to make it a forever kind of thing that terrified her. Some part of her clung to the idea that the vows themselves were the jinx.

"Erin, where's the financial section?"

"Hmmm?"

"The financial section," he repeated. "Is it over there?"

She riffled through the sections that were scattered on her side of the booth and handed him the business pages. How could one man make such a mess of a newspaper? When she finished with hers, the sections were all still neatly in order, while he had thrown parts of the paper all over the place to get to the Sunday magazine first. Then he'd read the sports, the front page, and the week-in-review section, dropping them on the floor, the table, or the seat beside him as he'd finished with each one.

Erin nibbled on a piece of toast as she watched a frown of concentration knit his brow. He was totally absorbed in what he was reading, automatically lifting bites of his pancakes to his mouth with amazing precision. She tried to imagine sitting across from him at breakfast just like this for the rest of her life. Her pulse accelerated in delighted approval of the image.

Suddenly the last section of the paper fluttered to the floor, and Mark put down his fork.

"Princess, you haven't touched your breakfast!"

Erin glanced down and realized that her eggs had congealed into a cold, unappetizing mass. She had taken one bite of her toast before abandoning it on the side of her plate.

"I guess I wasn't hungry."

Mark looked at her with concern. "What's wrong?"

"Nothing."

"Erin, something is obviously on your mind. Let's hear it. Does it have anything to do with us?"

She nodded. "Everyone is so sure you and I are right for each other. You. Maureen and Josh. The boys. Even my parents, and they haven't even met you. They're just going on what Josh and Maureen have told them."

"And you still have doubts."

"How can I not? Good Lord, it seemed like I had known Terry forever, and we still turned out to be a horrible mistake. I've only known you a week . . ."

"Nine days, if you count the day we met."

"Whatever. How can anybody be sure of anything in that amount of time?"

"You just have to look inside your heart."

"But my heart's not reliable."

"Oh, yes, it is. Your heart is always reliable," he said firmly.

"It wasn't with Terry."

"Are you so sure it was your heart that was talking back then?"

Erin regarded him quizzically. "What do you mean?"

"Weren't you looking for someone who would provide you with the sort of security you'd always felt was missing from your life?"

"I suppose so."

"Uh-uh. You know you were. And Terry seemed to fit all your preconceived ideas of what you needed in a man. It was as though you'd formulated a checklist and he met all the qualifications, so you decided to love him."

"Decided?"

"That's right. You were listening to your head, not your heart."

Erin's eyes widened at Mark's observation. Could he be right? That she'd talked herself into her feelings for Terry just because on the surface he'd seemed dependable? Had her head turned a mild infatuation into something more simply because he'd seemed to be the answer to her prayers for a reliable, responsible mate who would protect her from life's financial bumps and bruises?

"And," he said, forcing her attention away from the past and back to the present, back to him, "you're doing it again."

"I don't understand."

"You're listening to your head, which is making up all sorts of excuses why we can't possibly be right for each other. If you were listening to your heart, you'd know there's only one thing that matters: We love each other. If we believe in that, we can work out all the rest."

"That's an awfully simplistic approach. Lots of people who love each other have irreconcilable differences."

"You sound like a divorce lawyer, and by the time there are irreconcilable differences, whatever love there might have been is pretty well gone."

Erin sighed. "Okay, smart guy. Suppose, just suppose, that you're right. What am I supposed to do about it?"

"Tell that mind of yours to take a hike, and open up your heart. Your feelings will let you know what's right." He gave her a cocky grin as he deliberately brushed his leg provocatively against hers under the table. "My guess is that they already have."

"That's lust," she retorted.

"Oh?" Mark's eyebrows arched. "I had no idea you succumbed so easily to mere passion."

"I don't," she denied.

"Well, then . . ."

"Oh, forget it," she snapped in confusion. It was true. She had never felt so physically drawn to anyone, and their splendid lovemaking in the last forty-eight hours had gone far beyond the mere fulfillment of some sexual urge. There had been an intensity, a sharing of themselves that came only with a far deeper involvement. Love? Perhaps.

Listen to your heart, Erin. She gazed into Mark's eyes, noting their concern, the passionate fire that burned for her. For her. There was no doubt in her mind about that. As crazy as it seemed, Mark did love her. Suddenly she was as sure of that as she was of the eternal rise and fall of the tides. But did she dare to love him?

She sighed. To hear Josh and Maureen and even Mark tell it, she had no choice. It was already too late. Love had come when she was least expecting it, and, according to them, there wasn't a blessed thing she could do about it.

"So, princess. Shall we get on with it?"

"Get on with what?"

"Convincing that head of yours that your heart is very wise."

"Why do I have the feeling that you've mapped out a campaign that would make General MacArthur proud?"

"That's the only way to get what you want. You make a plan and go for it."

"But why me?"

"Because the minute I saw you, I wanted to protect

you, to cherish you forever. You had this vulnerable look in your eyes, and I wanted to know why. I wanted to fix whatever was wrong. When I saw you at the museum—"

"Wait a minute!" Erin interrupted. "Had you seen me before last Saturday?"

Mark looked decidedly uncomfortable. "Well . . . not exactly."

"What do you mean not exactly? Either you'd seen me before or you hadn't."

"Actually, I'd seen a picture of you."

"An ad?"

He nodded.

"Which one?"

"The one for Jasmine Cosmetics," he admitted at last.

"But how did you see it? It hasn't been released."

"I was doing some work for Jasmine. Someone had stolen one of their formulas. I happened to see the ad one day when I was up in the advertising area. I think I fell in love with you right then. When I saw you in person last Saturday, it was as if it were meant to be."

Erin was suddenly struck by something. "Are you sure you didn't arrange that meeting?"

"No. I had no idea you'd be there."

"But you knew who I was?"

"I'd asked around. It wasn't difficult."

"You investigated me?" she asked indignantly. "That took a lot of nerve."

"No, it didn't. I'm used to it."

"Well, I'm not."

"Don't get all upset, princess. I wasn't digging into your past or anything like that. I just asked who the lovely woman in the perfume campaign was. Any red-blooded male would have done that, given the opportunity. They were only too eager to tell me about their latest find. The more I heard, the more I wanted to know you. If I hadn't met you at the museum, I probably would have come looking for you."

"I suppose I should be grateful you told me. At least I finally understand how you were able to keep popping up in all the right places." She paused. "Tell me," she asked curiously, "would your infatuation have lasted this long if I'd gone along with you that very first day?"

He grinned at her and winked. "You'll never know, will you?"

"What happens when you realize the chase was better than the capture?"

"That will never happen. Once you and I are together, we'll make every day unpredictable and exciting and enchanting."

"I think you're in for a rude awakening."

"And I think you're confusing stability with boredom. Princess, I will always be there when you need me. You can count on it. That doesn't mean I won't turn up at noon one day and suggest we go roller-skating instead of having lunch or that I won't bring you wild-flowers when you were expecting roses. I want to keep you guessing about everything except my love for you."

"That's what worries me."

"How?"

"I don't want to guess whether we're going to be able to pay the bills or have a place to live."

Mark lifted her clenched hand from the table and brushed his lips across it. He forced her fingers open and kissed the palm, sending a jolt of electricity racing through her . . . straight to her heart. "Princess, I solemnly promise you those are things you'll never have to worry about. I will go to work for my father before I will ever let you spend a minute doing without a place to live or electricity or food."

The sincerity of Mark's promise touched Erin. That he would even mention the possibility of working for his father, when she knew how adamantly he was set against it, proved to her the depth of his concern for her need to feel secure.

"What about your father, Mark? Have you thought any more about going to see him?"

"I've thought about it," he said tersely.

"And?"

"Let's just drop it, shall we? Today is for us."

"Mark!"

"How would you like to go for a cruise?"

"I would like to meet your father."

Mark sighed and closed his eyes. A muscle in his jaw twitched nervously. At last he said reluctantly, "Maybe someday, Erin. Maybe someday."

Someday was awfully indefinite, but it was a major concession for him to make. And for now, she decided, that would have to do.

"Okay," she said cheerfully. "A cruise it is. Of course, you'll pardon me if I remain a bit skeptical. The last time you promised me a boat trip, we ended up in Central Park with a leaky toy sailboat."

"This time the boat will be bigger," he promised.

"But will it leak?"

"God, I hope not."

An hour later they were cruising around Manhattan amid a throng of tourists. Their gaze was being directed from the New Jersey shore and Frank Sinatra's hometown on their right to Wall Street on their left. The fading afternoon sunlight sparkled on the water, and Erin's breath caught in her throat at the sight of the Statue of Liberty. Despite her temporary attire of scaffolding, she was an impressively majestic lady.

For three hours they laughed at the Circle Line guide's irreverent tidbits about New York history and lifestyles. They exclaimed over the unexpected size of the island, which was so much bigger and more diverse than those jam-packed blocks of skyscrapers in midtown. And they held hands as twilight fell and shrouded the water in misty shades of blue and purple.

"You did it again," Erin said, gazing up at Mark with shining eyes as the boat drew into port.

"What's that, princess?"

"You gave me another magical day."

He shook his head. "It's not over yet. I have another surprise for you."

Erin's heart flipped over at the boyish excitement in his eyes. "What have you done now?"

"You'll see. Let's go home and change. I want to stop by my place first."

Erin was intrigued by Mark's apartment. The furniture was traditional bachelor, bland and uninteresting, but the personal touches were fascinating. There were souvenirs of trips out West, including an impressive painting by Remington and a collection of colorful Indian pottery. The bookshelves were filled with first editions of James Fenimore Cooper's works and photography books by Ansel Adams. An old rolltop desk that was oddly out of character with the rest of the furnishings was littered with paperwork. As Erin's gaze skimmed over the untidy mess, she spotted a faded color photograph shoved into one of the cubbyholes.

Unable to resist, she took the photo and held it up to the light. In it a woman with golden hair and a vibrant smile gazed proudly at a boy, a young man almost, in a football uniform. They were looking at each other with such love, such open affection, and such pride that the man in the picture seemed almost excluded from their private world. Mark and his parents. Erin wondered if his father was truly as remote as the picture seemed to indicate or if he'd been unintentionally shut out and simply had no idea how to get back into their lives.

"You ready?" Mark asked, coming up behind her and looking over her shoulder.

"Your mother was very beautiful," Erin said softly.

"Yes. She was," he agreed, his voice tight.

"Your father looks lonely."

Mark snorted. "Lonely? You've got to be kidding. He'd laugh in your face if you suggested such a thing."

"That doesn't mean it isn't true. Look at him in this picture. Try to see him objectively."

Mark snatched the picture from her hand and gazed at it. "I don't see it," he said, shoving the photo back into the desk.

"Mark?"

"Okay. So maybe he does look left out there. That doesn't mean he ever felt that way. He didn't feel anything."

Erin's eyebrow quirked meaningfully. "Maybe he's a little like me."

"What on earth do you mean?" Mark exploded. "He's not a thing like you."

"Maybe he was hurt so badly, he decided he didn't dare listen to his heart again." She reached up and circled her arms around Mark's neck and kissed him slowly and felt him tremble against her. At last she stepped back. "Think about it. Okay?"

He nodded, tried to say something, and couldn't.

Erin could see that he was struggling with the possibility that he'd been misjudging his father all these years.

"Come on, hero. You promised me a surprise," she said softly. "I want to see what it is."

He grinned finally at her excitement. "You're really getting into this now, aren't you?"

"You bet."

"Okay. Let's head over to your place."

During the ride across town to Erin's apartment, she tried to pry information out of Mark about the surprise.

"No way, princess. I'm not telling. Then it wouldn't be a surprise."

"I'm willing to sacrifice the surprise element."

"Uh-uh," he said adamantly. "You probably peeked into all your Christmas presents when you were a kid."

"Well," she admitted with an impish grin, "I was very good at getting the wrapping paper back the way it was when I found it."

"Yeah, but you must have had a lousy time on Christmas morning."

"Actually, no," she said, chuckling at the memory. "My parents learned of my treachery and started switching the tags on things they'd hidden. One year I was absolutely certain I was getting ice skates and a blue mohair sweater. They turned out to be for Maureen. I got a doll and a red sweater."

"I'm surprised you didn't get ashes and switches or a lump of coal."

"I think they considered it," she said as they climbed the stairs to her apartment. It took her several minutes to find her keys in the bottom of her purse and then unlock all the deadbolt locks she'd had installed. When she threw open the door at last, her eyes widened in amazement and delight.

The apartment was filled with flowers. It looked and smelled like a colorful spring garden, with bright-yellow daffodils, red tulips, purple irises, a bouquet of multihued pansies, and lilies of the valley. Classical music was playing low on the stereo, and the lights had been dimmed to create a romantic glow. In the center of the room a small table had been set with a damask tablecloth, a silver candleholder, and . . . a Monopoly board. Erin chuckled at the incongruity, the absolutely perfect whimsical touch that was pure Mark.

"Mark, it's . . . incredible," she said in an awed whisper. "How did you do it?"

"Magic, princess. Don't you believe in it yet?" he asked softly.

Erin gazed up at him, and her heart tripped wildly in her breast. "Yes," she murmured, coming into his open arms, her body yielding to his welcoming warmth. "I think I'm beginning to."

- *12* -

ERIN ROUSED HERSELF just slightly in the morning when Mark feathered a soft kiss across her lips and whispered good-bye. When he'd gone, she pulled his pillow into her arms so she could inhale the lingering scent of his cologne and pretend that he was still beside her. She was bathed in the incredible afterglow of his love. She felt radiant and amazingly secure and free of doubts. And she could hardly wait to see what he had in mind for today, the final day of his self-professed ten-day campaign to woo her.

She finally crawled out of bed at nine-thirty and began getting ready for her audition. Digging around in her closet for the perfect ensemble for the scandalous, manipulative character of Jennifer Torrance, a tough businesswoman whose arrival in town threatens to disrupt any number of lives, she found just what she was looking for. She pictured Jennifer as all style and flash and dazzle, so even though the scene was set in an office, she wore a black silk dress that skimmed over her curves, topped that with a long, draped silk jacket in bright canary yellow, and added a vibrant orange scarf. She left her hair hanging loose down her back in dark, shimmering, seductive waves.

Erin twirled around in front of the mirror and grinned. Jennifer Torrance was definitely a woman who had no self-doubts at all. She approached the world on her own confident terms—just as Mark did . . . and as she was finally beginning to again. As the thought flashed through her mind, Erin slowed and caught yet another image in the mirror. This time she saw the surprised look of a woman who had fallen crazily, happily-ever-after in love when she'd least expected it. But she also saw a woman who knew she could never turn back, who knew without the slightest reservation that she no longer wanted to, that she'd found a man who encouraged the best in her. The grin returned.

Filled with confidence and glowing with happiness, she did a little pirouette, then picked up her portfolio, the script for the audition, and her purse and dashed out the door. Her upbeat mood stayed with her all the way to the studio, upstaging her usual nervousness. She suffered only a tiny flicker of panic when she was introduced to Steve Reynolds, the soap's leading actor, and realized she would be playing a very volatile love scene with a complete stranger . . . the same love scene she had played out all too convincingly with Mark on Friday night.

"Don't worry about this," the suave, dark-haired actor said to her reassuringly as he walked with her onto the set. "You'll do just fine."

"I'm not worried," she answered blithely, smiling at

him brightly. The convincing lie was her first major piece of acting for the day.

He grinned back at her, revealing the dimple that set millions of hearts aflutter, and shrugged. "If you say so. Let's run through it a couple of times, and then Tricia can get it on tape."

With Tricia Brandon's clever directing and Steve's subtle encouragement, Erin flew through the scene without a hitch. Although she couldn't entirely banish the memory of her fiery rehearsal with Mark, she used that memory to her advantage, turning the few minutes of dialogue into a torrid scene that absolutely sizzled on the screen.

"Whew!" Steve said breathlessly when the taping ended. "You're something else, Erin Matthews!"

"I agree. You were terrific," Tricia seconded enthusiastically. "We'll get in touch with your agent, and I'm sure you'll be hearing from him later in the day."

But instead of basking in their praise and the virtual guarantee of a job, Erin found herself peering into the darkness at the back of the studio, hoping that Mark might be hidden in the shadows. When he didn't appear, she felt a sharp stab of disappointment. She'd started counting on him to turn up in the most unexpected places.

"Erin?"

"Hmm? What?" she said, focusing her attention back on the director. "I'm sorry. I guess I'm still coming down. That was a pretty intense scene."

"Thanks to you, it was," Tricia noted again. "I was just saying we'll be talking to your agent. I hope we can work things out."

"I hope so, too," Erin said sincerely. She liked both

Steve Reynolds and Tricia Brandon. Even more, she liked the idea of having a regular job for a change. Maybe Mark was her good luck charm in more ways than one.

On the way home, unsure of what his plans might be for the day, she shopped for groceries, splurging on steaks, vegetables for a salad, and baked potatoes. She even bought an expensive bottle of wine so they could celebrate her new job and their new love.

"Don't get carried away," she warned herself. "The job isn't yours yet."

But the love was, and nothing was going to put a damper on her excitement as she busied herself in the kitchen and waited for the phone to ring. When she'd completed all the advance preparations for dinner, she took a long, hot bubble bath, then put on a bright red T-dress that hugged her every slender curve. Despite its inexpensive simplicity, it was a sexy dress, and she knew Mark would like it. She could envision the appreciative, possessive gleam in his eyes as he surveyed her from head to toe.

As soon as she was dressed, she settled back on the sofa with a magazine. When the phone rang a little after five, she snatched it up.

"Hi, doll," her agent announced. "You knocked 'em dead over there. If you want the part, you've got it."

Erin's initial disappointment at not finding Mark on the line gave way to excitement. "Murray, that's wonderful. Is it a good deal?"

"Would I get you any other kind?" he chided her affectionately. "I take it you want the job."

"Absolutely. When do I start?"

"Two weeks."

"That soon?" It was amazing how quickly her life was changing.

"What's the matter? You have something more important to do?"

Erin chuckled. Murray should only know about the plans Mark had in mind for her. "Nothing I can talk about now. I'll be there in two weeks."

"Okay, kid. I'll get the contract over to you in the morning for your signature."

"Thanks, Murray. You're wonderful."

"Of course I am," he retorted. "See ya, kid."

Erin sat back on the sofa and tried to figure out what she was feeling. Excitement. Anticipation. A touch of anxiety. But most of all she was feeling an odd stirring of disappointment that Mark was not here to share this triumph with her. Where was he? He should have been here by now or at least called. After nine days of such intensity, this unexpected lull was disturbing, especially on a day so critical to this crazy campaign of his.

Recalling Maureen's advice about not suffering in silence, she picked up the phone and dialed his apartment. There was no answer. She tried the company where he'd been working for the last few weeks, but the secretary told her he'd been out since mid-morning.

"Where on earth could he be?" she murmured aloud, a tiny frown creasing her forehead. She snapped her fingers as a thought struck her. "Jean-Pierre's. Of course. He's gone to help him again."

As the thought crossed her mind, a tiny shiver of dread raced through her. If he was with Jean-Pierre, it meant there had been more trouble. For the next hour she called the artist's studio and kept getting a busy signal. Finally, thoroughly frustrated and growing more nervous by the minute, she had the operator check the line.

"I'm sorry, ma'am. That number appears to be out of order. I'll report it."

"I don't want it reported. I want to get through," she snapped irrationally.

"There's nothing I can do. They'll have it checked out as soon as possible."

"Okay. Thank you," she said resignedly.

Now what? She could either wait here and hope Mark would show up eventually, or she could go looking for him. She decided any action at all would be better than sitting here working herself into a state. Besides, he might need help. She turned on her answering machine, grabbed her coat, and ran downstairs. Wishing Josh would materialize, she searched frantically for a taxi, finally finding an empty one several blocks away.

She gave the driver the address where Josh had taken her the week before and sat on the edge of the seat for the entire trip, trying to convince herself that her imagination was simply working overtime, that Mark wasn't really in any danger. But a sixth sense told her he was. It was more than just the events with Jean-Pierre's gang of thieves that convinced her she was right. It was an intuitive feeling in the pit of her stomach, as though her ESP had tuned into Mark and seen him pitted against some evil force.

"Don't be ridiculous," she snapped.

"You say something, lady?"

"Just giving myself some advice," she replied as the cab pulled to a stop in front of Jean-Pierre's studio. Glancing out, she noticed that the door was open but no light was on, even though it had been dark for the last hour. Her stomach tightened. "Could you wait for me?" she asked the driver.

"Lady, as long as this meter's running, I can do anything you want."

"Then stay here while I go inside, please."

The driver looked over his shoulder at her, then looked toward the darkened doorway. "Maybe I'd better go with you."

Though Erin hated admitting to her nervousness, there was something reassuring about the idea of being accompanied into Jean-Pierre's studio. She approached the door cautiously and peered inside. Feeling around for a light switch, she finally found it and flipped it on, bathing the studio in a stark glare. Unlike last week, it had a deserted feeling about it, even though several of his larger works were still in place.

"What are we looking for, lady?"

"I'm trying to locate a friend of mine."

"Doesn't look to me like anybody's here."

It didn't look that way to Erin, either, but she wasn't giving up yet. Perhaps there was some clue to where Mark and Jean-Pierre had gone. When she opened the door to the tiny apartment Jean-Pierre kept in the back, she gasped in dismay. The place had been thoroughly ransacked, with clothes and papers left scattered about.

"Whew! Some mess!" the taxi driver muttered behind her. "Lady, maybe this wasn't such a good idea. How about I take you back home?"

"Not yet," Erin said stubbornly, walking around the room looking for something that might help guide her to Mark and Jean-Pierre. But what? What was she looking for? Even searching for a needle in a haystack would be easier than this, she decided wearily. At least you knew you were looking for a needle.

When she spotted the little trail of red dots on the floor, her breath caught in her throat. Bending down, she tentatively touched it.

"Let it be paint," she murmured under her breath. "Please let it be paint."

It wasn't. She resisted the urge to scream. When the cab driver leaned over her shoulder to see what she'd found, she jumped nervously.

"Sorry, lady. I thought you knew I was right behind you."

"It's okay. I guess I'm more frightened than I'd realized."

"Then let's get out of here."

"In a minute," Erin promised, standing up and following the trail of blood toward a door she hadn't noticed before. "I just want to see where this goes."

It opened onto an alley, which appeared deserted except for a collection of battered garbage cans and a plump cat that obviously knew how to scavenge for food. It meowed pitifully at the sight of Erin and wound itself through her legs.

"Sorry, fellow, you're on your own," she said, rubbing his head absentmindedly as she tried to figure out what to do next. Surely there was a certain amount of logic to this investigating business, and she was as logical as the next person. Unfortunately she had very little to go on. It was as though she'd been given only two or three pieces of a giant puzzle, all of them sky blue, and then been asked to figure out what was in the rest of the picture.

Admit it, she told herself. It's hopeless. You might as well go home and wait.

As she started to walk back into the main part of the

studio, she heard a car screech to a halt outside. Her heart thudded, and her palms turned sweaty. She looked at the cab driver with anxious eyes, and he motioned for her to slip back out of sight. He waited beside the door.

First a long, hulking shadow fell across the floor. Erin held her breath. When the man finally stepped through the doorway, the taxi driver caught him from behind.

"What the hell?" The words echoed through the studio, followed by a string of oaths that sounded all too familiar. The breath Erin had been holding whooshed out of her in relief.

"Josh! What are you doing here?"

"Lady, you know this man?"

"My brother-in-law," she said succinctly.

"Erin, are you out of your mind? What the hell are you doing here? And who is this?"

"No. I am not crazy. I'm looking for Mark. And this nice gentleman is the cab driver who brought me here." She grinned at Josh. "Did I cover everything?"

"You could have gotten yourself killed," Josh muttered, his large hands on her shoulders. Erin had the feeling he was only barely resisting the urge to shake her.

"By the way, what are you doing here?"

"Mark had a feeling you might have come down here. He asked me to come after you."

"You've talked to Mark? Where is he? What's wrong?"

"He's at the hospital."

Erin's knees went weak. The blood. It had been Mark's. He was hurt. "The hospital? Is he okay?"

"Obviously he's okay, since I talked to him," Josh retorted impatiently.

"Don't you snap at me, Josh Lawrence. I've been scared out of my wits ever since I found that blood in the back room, and then you announce Mark's in the hospital as casually as if he were taking a stroll. I don't think it's totally illogical on my part to think he might have been injured."

"Sorry, kiddo," he apologized. "Mark is fine. It's Jean-Pierre who's been hurt. Apparently there was another brush with the vandals, only this time they decided to go after him instead of one of his works."

"Why?"

Josh shrugged. "You'll have to ask Mark about that. I'll take you over to the hospital now."

"I take it you don't need me anymore, lady."

"No, but thank you very much. I don't know what I'd have done if you hadn't been here with me."

"You'd have landed a karate chop on me yourself," Josh retorted dryly. "Frankly, I'm glad I only tangled with him."

The driver looked at Erin quizzically. "You know karate?"

She shrugged. "I took a class or two."

"A class or two, humph!" Josh looked at her indignantly. His eyes twinkled as he faced the other driver. "Black belt."

"Hell, lady, you should have been protecting me."

Erin grinned at him. "There was no need. You had things under control."

They shut the studio up tightly, paid the other driver, and then climbed into Josh's taxi. As he whisked her the few blocks to the hospital, Josh gave her a nonstop lecture on leaping without looking. "You had no business going over there."

"I had to see if Mark was okay."

"And endangered yourself in the process. A lot of good that would have done Mark."

"Like you just told the taxi driver, I can take care of myself if I have to. Those classes you object to do serve a purpose, you know."

"That's not the point."

"Oh, yes, it is. I was not going to sit around in my apartment like some ninny and just wait for Mark to turn up. I knew he was in some kind of trouble, and he might have needed my help."

"What he needed was to know you were safely at home waiting for him. The man almost flipped out when he started calling and you weren't there."

"Why didn't he just assume I'd gone to a class or something? Why did he automatically think I'd gone chasing after him?"

"Because he knows how your mind works."

"That's what he thinks," Erin muttered under her breath.

"What did you say?"

"I said Mark Townsend is getting awfully cocky."

Josh grinned at her. "I'd say he has reasonable cause."

"Oh, is that so?"

"That's so, kiddo. Your actions are giving you away."

When the cab pulled up at the emergency entrance, Erin jumped out. She stopped to glare down at Josh. "You men always stick together, don't you?"

His eyes twinkled back at her. "When's the wedding?" he taunted.

"Don't hold your breath," she snapped back, stalking through the doors as the deep rumble of Josh's laughter trailed after her.

All her tough resolve faded as she approached the desk in the emergency room. What if Josh had only been protecting her? What if Mark had been injured? Would she be able to bear it? The thought of him lying on some stretcher, wounded, made the color drain from her face.

"I'm looking for Mark Townsend," she told the nurse behind the desk.

"Over there," she responded, pointing toward a waiting room, crowded with injured people and their nervous companions.

Erin's gaze flew around the room until at last she saw him. He was sitting on one of the uncomfortable plastic chairs, his hair mussed, his complexion practically gray from exhaustion. He was holding a coffee cup in one shaking hand. He looked terrible.

She walked over to him and dropped down beside him, putting her hand on his knee. "Hi," she said softly. "You okay?"

His eyes brightened immediately, and his hand reached out to caress her face. "Princess. Josh found you."

"Yes, the rescue mission was successful."

"Rescue mission?" His voice immediately filled with concern, and his glance raked over her. "Are you okay?"

"I'm fine, now that I know you're all right."

"I'm sorry I worried you, princess. It's been a hell of a day."

"What happened?"

"We finally caught the guys who've been after Jean-Pierre. Unfortunately, not before they managed to rough him up a little."

"How's he doing?"

"He'll be fine, as soon as they take a few stitches in his hand."

"In his hand?" she repeated in a horrified whisper.

"Oh, princess, don't look like that. It's not bad."

"He'll be able to work again?"

"So they say."

"But why were these guys after him?"

"One of them was a former apprentice, who started getting ugly after Jean-Pierre fired him for stealing things. He had the help of a few of his less savory pals."

"How did you know that's who it was?"

"Too many of the things that happened could only have been done by someone who knew Jean-Pierre's work very well and knew exactly which pieces to destroy and how to do it so that they would be beyond repair."

"That's awful."

"Yes. Well, luckily for Jean-Pierre, we caught them before the whole situation got completely out of control. Tonight was only planned as a warning that he was going to be in danger himself. The guy seemed to think that would make him consider rehiring him."

"Which, of course, he had no intention of doing."

"None."

"Are these guys in jail?"

"For the time being."

Erin shuddered.

"How about some coffee, princess? It tastes like mud, but it'll keep you awake."

"I'm not sleepy. I've had enough excitement tonight to keep my adrenaline pumping for a month."

"That's good," he said, his eyes burning into her until she felt suddenly breathless.

"It is?"

"Absolutely, because I have no intention of letting the tenth day of my campaign end like this."

Erin grinned at the blatantly suggestive promise. "You might want to reconsider that."

"Oh?" he said blankly. "Why?"

"You may have trouble topping what's already happened. I've certainly never had another day quite like this."

"Oh, I think I can manage to make you forget all about today," he said softly as his finger played across her lips. She nipped the finger playfully, then drew it into her mouth in a provocative gesture.

"Then I dare you to start trying now," she taunted, her blood already flowing through her like molten lava.

He sat back and winked at her. "Patience, princess. We have all night."

- *13* -

ONCE JOSH HAD driven Jean-Pierre back to his studio and Mark had checked to make sure the locks were secure, they drove on to Erin's.

"Would you like some coffee before you head for home?" Erin offered.

Before Josh could respond, Mark stepped in. "It's late," he said significantly. "I'm sure Josh wants to get back to Maureen."

"A cup of coffee won't take that long."

"Erin!"

"It's the least we can do."

"I don't suppose either of you would care to hear from me?" Josh asked innocently.

Two sets of flashing eyes stared at him.

"That's better," he said lightly. "I'll be running along now. Mark's right. I do need to get home. You two enjoy the rest of the evening."

"Night, Josh," Erin said, glowering at Mark.

"See you tomorrow, kiddo."

"A wise man, your brother-in-law," Mark noted as the cab pulled away.

"Humph!"

"Don't you flash those eyes at me, young lady. We have some unfinished business to take care of."

"It could have waited a half hour, for goodness' sake," Erin argued.

Mark's arms went around her possessively, and Erin found herself securely locked against the radiating heat of his body. His lips nipped at her earlobe and brushed light kisses along the column of her neck. His tongue touched her lips, which promptly parted on an eager sigh. It was an extraordinarily provocative way to win an argument. It was, she decided, cheating, but she couldn't think of a single thing to do to defend herself against it.

"Say that again," he challenged.

"What?" she said softly, all thoughts of anything except Mark and the gentle touch of his lips on hers having suddenly fled.

"Tell me again that this could have waited."

Erin buried her face in his chest and pressed her hips more tightly into his as a shudder of desire tore through her. "Maybe for another minute," she choked out breathlessly.

"How long?" he teased as his fingers found the sensitive spot just below the curve of her breast.

"Okay, okay," she conceded with a laugh. "Not another second."

Mark suddenly released her. "That's better," he said with satisfaction.

"Hey," she protested. "Where do you think you're going?"

"Upstairs," he said dryly, then gave her a daring grin. "Unless you were planning on our making a spectacle of ourselves right here on the street."

"I doubt if anyone would notice. They certainly don't pay any attention to muggings."

"Hey, I'm willing to stay here and find out, if you are."

She caught the challenge in his eyes and backed down. "Never mind."

They trudged up the stairs to Erin's apartment, and when they reached the door and unlocked it, Mark suddenly swept her off her feet and into his arms.

"You lunatic, put me down," she demanded as he kicked open the door.

"Not a chance. This was supposed to be our wedding day, remember? Since we've had to postpone the wedding, the least I can do is carry you over the threshold."

"So," Erin teased, "we're back to that again, are we?"

"Princess, I never left it. If it hadn't been for Jean-Pierre, today would have been a spectacular windup to my campaign. You wouldn't have been able to resist walking down that aisle with me at sunset."

"Oh, really?" she taunted, her pulse skipping erratically. "What exactly did you have in mind?"

"First I was going to hire a limousine to whisk you off to the top of the World Trade Center for lunch. We were going to have champagne and caviar on the way. Then, after lunch, while you were at your audition—How did that go, by the way?"

"Don't stop now."

"But I want to hear about the audition."

"I got the part," she confessed, smiling at him. "I think it had something to do with all that rehearsing."

Mark gave her a dazzling grin. "I'm sure," he said dryly. "Oh, princess, that's wonderful! I'm so proud of you." He gave her a congratulatory kiss, a thoroughly unsatisfying peck on the cheek. Erin wound her arms around his neck and pulled his head back down to hers, her interest in his campaign strategy forgotten.

"Uh-uh," she whispered against his lips. "You're not getting away with that paltry excuse for a kiss, Mark Townsend. For a man who's trying to win my heart, you're not being very convincing."

"Oh?" he chuckled. "Just what would I have to do to convince you?"

"This," she suggested softly, her mouth capturing his and her tongue slipping inside to engage in a passionate duel with his. Her hands were busy as well, tugging his shirt from his slacks, then sliding inside to splay across the warm, supple skin of his back. She could feel the ripple of tension in his muscles, the taut responsiveness.

"And this," she added, as one hand massaged and taunted, while the other slipped lower to caress the tight, tempting curve of his bottom. He moaned and rubbed against her until her breasts and the mound that shielded her femininity were swollen and aching with white-hot desire.

"Is that how you kissed that actor?" he asked curiously.

"What?" Erin asked groggily. "Where did that come from? Don't tell me you're jealous."

"Of course not," he denied. When Erin's eyebrow shot up disbelievingly, he said, "Well, maybe just a little. I was just wondering if your acting was that realistic."

"I don't know. It was . . . just a kiss. It didn't mean anything," she said, pushing aside the image of how that kiss had apparently sizzled on the screen. There was no need to tell Mark about the impact it had had on Tricia and Steve, that the love scene alone had probably convinced them to hire her.

Mark looked at her closely, as though trying to read her thoughts. Erin prayed he couldn't read her mind yet. It was bad enough that he could track her like a deer-slayer.

"Are you sure?" he asked.

"Absolutely," she said solemnly, adding honestly, "Nobody kisses like you do."

"Oh, really?" His voice perked up, and he was suddenly gloating, positively gloating.

"I'm glad to see your ego didn't suffer too long," she quipped. "Now, tell me what else you had in mind for today."

"After the audition, I was going to take you to the zoo, where I had trained one of the parrots to say 'I love you. Will you marry me?'"

"Sure."

"I swear to you."

"Mark, if you'd been at the zoo trying to teach the parrots to talk, you'd be locked away in Bellevue by now."

He shook his head. "May I remind you that this is New York."

"Even in New York, you don't get a parrot to propose for you."

"Okay, spoilsport," he conceded. "So, I was going to ask you myself."

"And if I'd said yes?"

"Then I'd have whisked you off to a church so fast you'd have gotten dizzy."

"I think you're the one who's dizzy. You have to have a license before you can get married."

"A minor detail. I have very cooperative friends in some very strategic jobs at City Hall."

"What about the church? And my dress? And somebody to sing? And my family?"

"I reserved the church the day we met. I bought the dress last week. I have a friend who has agreed to sing. And your family has been on call for days. All we have to do is say the word."

"You've thought of everything."

He nodded proudly. "Your bouquet's on order, too."

"And rings. I suppose you have those?"

"In my pocket."

Erin looked at him skeptically. "You don't really?"

"Check it out."

She felt carefully in the pockets of his jacket.

"Not there," he taunted, his eyes glittering like gleaming silver.

Gently she patted the pockets of his jeans, noting the tension in his face as she deliberately lingered over the search. "Hmm," she teased. "Not here. What about here?"

"Erin, please!"

"Oh, am I disturbing you?" she asked innocently.

"Damn right, you're disturbing me," he growled as his lips came down on hers hungrily.

"Mark! The rings."

"To hell with the rings."

"But you can't get married without rings."

He looked at her cautiously.

"Meaning?"

"What do you think?"

"Don't play word games with me. What are you saying?"

"I'm saying that a smart prince would have his timing down and know when to ask a princess to marry him."

"Ah," he said softly. "I see."

He dropped dramatically to one knee. "Erin Matthews, will you do me the honor of becoming my princess forever?"

She studied him consideringly. "What about my dowry?"

"I'll waive that requirement."

"Will I like it in your kingdom?"

"I think you're going to love it in my kingdom," he replied softly, pulling her down on top of him. "So, what about it?"

"Only if you promise never to put me through another night like this one."

He shook his head. "I won't make promises I can't keep, princess. I can only promise to love you more and more each day for the rest of our lives."

Erin sighed happily. "I'd say that's a pretty good promise."

"So when's the wedding?"

"Since you've managed to take care of most of the details, how about Saturday? Our second anniversary."

"Princess, you're beginning to think like I do!" he exclaimed with delight.

"I know, and it scares the daylights out of me."

"Don't be scared. It just proves what I've been telling you all along."

"Which is?"

"That we're perfectly compatible."

"Or perfectly nuts."

His hands skimmed over her until a wildfire raged inside. "For tonight, let's just work on compatible."

- *14* -

THE DAY OF the wedding dawned clear and bright, another incredible fall day. When Erin rolled over in bed and found that Mark wasn't there, a ripple of fear washed over her—until she remembered his reluctant departure the night before, right after they had made love...the second time. He'd tried to leave earlier, explaining as he pulled on his clothes, "It's bad luck for the groom to see the bride on the day of the wedding."

"That's ridiculous," she'd protested, trying to lure him back beside her. He ducked out of her arms and out of her reach.

"It may be," he retorted, "but I'm not taking any chances with our wedding. We're doing this one by the book."

Erin laughed at the perfectly outrageous comment. "Since when? If this has been your idea of doing things by the book, I'm not sure the world is ready for what you'd do when you want to get a little wild."

Mark grinned sheepishly. "Okay. So maybe we've been a little unorthodox about the courtship," he admitted. "It's about time we started following the rules."

"Don't go stuffy on me now," she teased, using one of his favorite lines and snatching his jeans and holding them behind her back.

"Give me my pants," he ordered.

She shook her head. "Your tyrant act doesn't scare me. You want 'em, come and get 'em."

"Erin!"

He'd glowered at her, then climbed back into the bed and tussled with her for the jeans. Just as she'd anticipated, their battle had quickly escalated into passion, and he had shown her once more just how far he was from being stuffy or ordinary. It had been after midnight when he'd finally left, ignoring Erin's protest that since it was already technically the day of the wedding, he might as well stay.

She stretched and yawned. She felt wonderful, as though a whole wonderful, exciting world had been spread out before her and she'd been given her choice of anything in it. And she had chosen well. She had chosen Mark.

Or rather, he had chosen her. She'd just been swept along by that rampaging tide of his emotions until she'd seen that their relationship was perfect for her as well. And it was perfect. She felt safe and secure and, most important of all, loved. Very much loved.

Her whole family had seen that. Her parents had taken to Mark immediately when they'd finally met him the day after she'd accepted his proposal. They didn't appear the least disconcerted by the whirlwind courtship and had accepted him as enthusiastically as they had

Josh years earlier. When she'd asked them why, her
mother had smiled complacently and said, "Why,
honey, because it's so obvious the man's in love with
you and you're in love with him. Nothing else matters."

One thing did, Erin thought sadly. She still wished
that Mark's father could be included in all of this. She
hadn't been able to get the image of that lonely man in
the snapshot out of her mind. She had tried nudging
Mark again several times over the last few days and had
thought she was making progress, but last night when
they'd talked about the small guest list for the wedding,
he hadn't said a word about his father.

She sighed. She could call Mr. Townsend herself, but
Mark would probably be furious with her. Even if he
came to understand her interference at some point in the
future, it might very well spoil their wedding day.
Before she could decide whether it was worth the risk,
the phone rang.

"Hi, princess!"

Her heart flipped over, and a soft smile tilted her
lips. "Mark."

"Only a few more hours and you'll be mine," he
whispered huskily, sending an excited shiver along
Erin's spine. Romantic to the very end, Mark had
arranged for their wedding to take place at the precise
moment they had met. He might very well have held it
on the steps of the Metropolitan Museum as well, but
Erin had held out for a small chapel near Gramercy Park
where she often attended services.

"No second thoughts?"

"Not a one. You?"

"None," she said confidently. "Um, Mark?"

"Yes."

"Where are we going on our honeymoon?"

He chuckled. "Away."

"That's no answer."

"It's the only one you're going to get."

"But, Mark, how can I pack if I don't know where we're going?"

"You're not packing. Maureen is."

"Is she going, too?" she asked sarcastically.

"Very funny," he retorted. "Princess, this is going to be a surprise."

"I hate surprises," she grumbled.

"Only because you feel left out."

"Well, of course. That's what a surprise is. Everybody else is in on all the fun except you."

"Ah, but you get to go on the honeymoon. They don't. I guarantee you that'll be more fun than planning it."

She sighed. "I suppose."

"What do you mean, you suppose?" he demanded indignantly. "This is going to be one knock'em dead honeymoon, the best ever, a trip to the stars."

"We're going to the Milky Way?"

Mark moaned. "No. I can honestly tell you we are not going to the Milky Way, so you can leave your Darth Vader Halloween costume at home."

"Too bad. It would have been something to remember."

"It will be something to remember."

"If you say so."

"Princess, don't get that sad little tremor in your voice. I am not telling! In fact, I am going to get off this phone right now."

Erin chuckled. "That means I'm getting to you.

Come on, tell. Please. I'll act surprised when we get on the plane."

"Who said anything about a plane?" Mark replied. "Bye, princess."

"Mark!"

"See you in church."

"Maybe," Erin muttered as the receiver clicked in her ear. The phone rang again almost instantly.

"What do you mean maybe?"

"You don't have an exclusive on surprises, Mark Townsend," she taunted and hung up.

When the phone rang again, she ignored it. She stepped into the shower and turned the water on full force so she couldn't hear the ringing. "Serves him right," she muttered gleefully, then burst happily into the chorus of "Get Me to the Church on Time."

She'd just finished a light lunch when Maureen arrived to help her get ready. She was carrying a brand-new suitcase.

"I hear you're packing for the honeymoon," Erin commented.

"It's already done."

Erin regarded her quizzically. "How?"

"Mark bought a few things, and I packed them. You just need to put your toothbrush and a few things like that in an overnight bag and you'll be all set."

Erin eagerly grabbed the suitcase and flopped it onto the sofa. But when she tried to open it, the clasps wouldn't budge. "It's locked."

Maureen grinned at her obvious disappointment. "That's right."

"Okay, so what's the combination?"

Her sister shrugged. "Beats me."

"But you must know."

"Uh-uh. Mark wouldn't tell me."

"Blast him."

"He is one very determined man. He said something about this not being like all those Christmases. Any idea what he meant?"

Erin collapsed on the sofa and whacked the suitcase in frustration. "Oh, I know what he meant all right. Never again will I tell him any little secrets from my past."

Maureen chuckled delightedly. "Ah-ha. You told him about peeking at your presents."

"Yes," Erin muttered. "He now seems to think it is his duty to keep me off-guard for the rest of my life by springing surprises on me."

"I had the feeling he was springing surprises on you from the day you met."

"Now that you mention it, yes, he was."

"That's part of what intrigued you about him, isn't it?"

"Yes."

"And you've been having fun?"

Erin grinned at her. "I see your point. I guess I should just let him do his thing."

"It's certainly worked so far."

"Okay." She gazed up at Maureen. "You're sure you don't have the combination, though?"

"Erin!"

"Okay, okay. I'll forget it and get ready."

Practically the instant the two of them had finished dressing, the doorbell rang to announce the arrival of the rest of the family.

"Hey, kiddo, you look beautiful. The second prettiest

bride I've ever seen," Josh announced, giving her a hug.

"You look great, Aunt Erin. You, too, Mom," Robby added loyally.

Jeb and Todd seemed to be awed by the formal clothes everyone was wearing. They perched uncomfortably on the edge of the sofa and watched while the grown-ups sipped champagne supplied by Erin's father.

"Happy, puddin'?" he asked.

Erin raised shining eyes to meet her father's proud gaze.

"Very happy, Dad."

"Mark's a fine man."

"I think so, too."

He glanced at his watch. "And we'd better not keep him waiting. He'll be a wreck over at the church all by himself."

"Jean-Pierre is with him."

"All the more reason to hurry. I've seen that crazy stuff of his. I'd hate for some of his wild ideas to rub off on that nice, sensible man of yours."

"Sensible?" Erin repeated dryly. It was not a description she would have chosen for her future husband.

"Of course, he's sensible. He's marrying one of the two prettiest, nicest women in the world, isn't he?"

"Thanks, Dad." She regarded him closely. "You're sure you don't mind that this has happened so fast?"

"Puddin', love's like a bolt of lightning. It can change things in an instant. Your mama and I may have waited to get married, but I knew the day I first saw her she was the only woman in the world for me. I'm only sorry I haven't been able to give her the world like I promised back then."

"Don't you worry about that, Thomas Matthews," Erin's mother chided softly. "I've had the happiest thirty-five years any woman could want. Even in the bad times I knew you loved me, and there's no greater gift than that."

Erin could see that love shining in their eyes as they gazed at each other, and she hoped that she and Mark would still have that kind of glow about them when they'd been married thirty-five years. Of course, that wasn't likely to happen if they didn't all get moving and get to the church.

The ride over took only a few minutes, and when they got there, Erin waited in the car while Josh checked to make sure the few guests had arrived and that Mark and Jean-Pierre were ready. Then he escorted her mother to her place and seated the boys with her.

At last it was time to begin.

From the back of the church, Erin saw Mark and Jean-Pierre enter through a side door. The organist began the wedding march, and Maureen started down the aisle. As Erin and her father started to follow, she saw that there was another guest, sitting on the groom's side of the church in the front row. Even from the back, she could tell that it had to be Mark's father. The shape of the head was the same; the set of the shoulders was touchingly familiar.

As she passed the pew where he was seated, she paused for just a fraction of a second and looked at Mr. Townsend. The gentle, grateful smile he gave her filled her heart to overflowing. She could tell from that look that he had made peace with his son at last and the ghost of loneliness she had seen in that photograph had been banished forever.

She took the final few steps down the aisle and looked up into Mark's eyes, her own eyes shimmering with tears.

The brilliant smile on his face faded instantly, and his eyes clouded with concern. "Princess, you're crying," he whispered.

She nodded, reaching out to touch him reassuringly. "It's okay. I'm just so happy."

Mark's lips curved in a smile that was reminiscent of the one she'd just seen on his father's face. "You recognized him, then?"

"I knew the moment I saw him," she said. "And I'm very proud of you."

"What else could I do, princess? Today is for family."

"Yes. It is . . . for *our* family."

He grinned at her. "Then please stop crying before they all think you're having second thoughts and demand that we call the whole thing off."

"No way," she said, her eyes shining up at him. She placed her hand in his and held on tightly. "They'd have to drag me out of here. I have every intention of living happily ever after . . ." She paused, then added softly, "With my prince."

- *Epilogue* -

"MARK, I FEEL as though I could reach out and touch the stars."

"Isn't that what I promised you for your honeymoon, princess?"

"But a hot air balloon in France . . . I never expected that."

"You like it, though?"

"It's wonderful. It's like floating on air. There's just one thing . . ."

"What's that?"

"When do we really get to the honeymoon?"

"This is the honeymoon."

"No. I mean the . . . you know . . . *the honeymoon.*"

"Ohhhh. You mean this part?"

"Mmmm."

"And this?"

"Yes."

"And maybe this?"

"Oh, Mark . . . Mark! The basket is tilting!"

"So it is. Maybe this isn't such a good idea. Can you be patient just a few more minutes?"

"How many minutes?"

"A few. Why don't you close your eyes?"

"And miss the view? No way."

"Close 'em."

"Lordy, you're bossy."

"You can open them now."

"Can't you make up your mind? Ohhhh! Just look at the lights. Mark, it's a castle."

"Actually, it's a chateau."

"That's where we're going? A castle . . . chateau . . . whatever?"

"Where else would a princess spend her honeymoon?"

"Mark, you're incredible."

"Of course. Isn't that why you married me?"

"Nope."

"It isn't? I'm crushed."

"I married you because I love you."

"Oh."

"But I love you because you're incredible."

"Princess, you're crazy."

"I thought that was what you wanted."

"It was."

"Then we both got exactly what we wanted, didn't we?"

"We sure did."

SECOND CHANCE AT LOVE

COMING NEXT MONTH

TANGLING WITH WEBB #346 by Laine Allen
Writer's block drives whimsical Cristy McKnight
to a rash wager with wickedly handsome, infuriatingly
smug Webster Cannon: She'll concoct his
mystery if he'll pen her romance!

FRENCHMAN'S KISS #347 by Kerry Price
So what if he makes beautiful music, cooks
divinely, and kisses exquisitely? Thoroughly
unpredictable French composer Jean-Claude Delacroix
is *not* the reliable companion Sherry Seaton requires.

KID AT HEART #348 by Aimée Duvall
Where toy designer Lisa Fleming goes,
chaos follows—to the chagrin…and delight…
of toy company owner Chase Sanger, who begins
to hope he's found a lifelong playmate!

MY WILD IRISH ROGUE #349 by Helen Carter
Darkly handsome, joyfully spontaneous,
Liam Claire teases and tempts reserved Ingrid Peterson,
pursuing her across Ireland until she's nervous,
confused…and *very* aroused!

HAPPILY EVER AFTER #350 by Carole Buck
Lily Bancroft will do anything to get
the money—even dress as Snow White—but nothing
on earth will ever turn ruthlessly powerful
Dylan Chase into a fairy-tale prince.

TENDER TREASON #351 by Karen Keast
Wealthy, elusive, dictatorial Nyles Ryland electrifies
insurance investigator Lauren Kane with silken caresses
and drugging kisses. But she has no intention of playing
this week's lover to Grand Cayman's mystery man…

SECOND CHANCE AT LOVE

Be Sure to Read These New Releases!

SWANN'S SONG #334 by Carole Buck
Knowing both karate and kids, Megan Harper poses
as a nanny to secretly guard rock star Colin Swann and
his irrepressible son...and gets into deep
trouble when love complicates the deception!

STOLEN KISSES #335 by Liz Grady
Mattie Hamilton is rehearsing a museum
heist when tuxedo-clad thief Devlin Seamus Devlin
tackles her in midair...and offers to tutor
her in *all* kinds of midnight maneuvers!

GOLDEN GIRL #336 by Jacqueline Topaz
In sophisticated Hollywood, schoolteacher Olivia Gold
finds both her movie star grandmother *and* dashing soulmate
Andrew Carr—who transforms her into a glittering
golden girl and spellbinds her with sensual enchantment.

SMILES OF A SUMMER NIGHT #337 by Delaney Devers
Like a modern rogue, plantation owner
Jules Robichaux sweeps April Jasper away with cynical
charm, smoothly seduces her under moonlit
magnolias...but won't trust her enough to offer his love.

DESTINY'S DARLING #338 by Adrienne Edwards
"Bought" by ex-husband Bart Easton at a charity
benefit, Dot Biancardi recalls poignant moments—of
gallant courtship, wedded bliss...and lonely
heartache. Dare she risk repeating past mistakes?

WILD AND WONDERFUL #339 by Lee Williams
Trapped on a wild Maine island with brawny recluse
Greg Bowles, who's rejected the inheritance she's come to
give him, heir hunter Alicia Saunders finds a new
tension building...desire quickening.

Order on opposite page

A STIRRING PAGEANTRY
OF
HISTORICAL ROMANCE